Snakehead

Super Sleuth

Star Pilot   Super Bug

 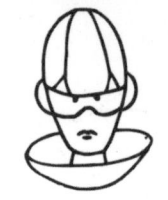 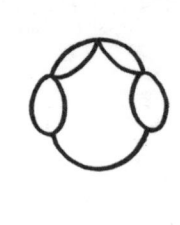 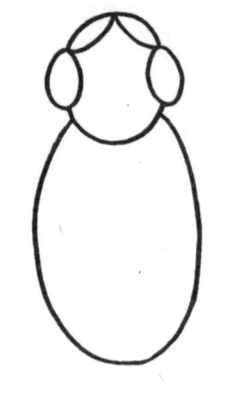

 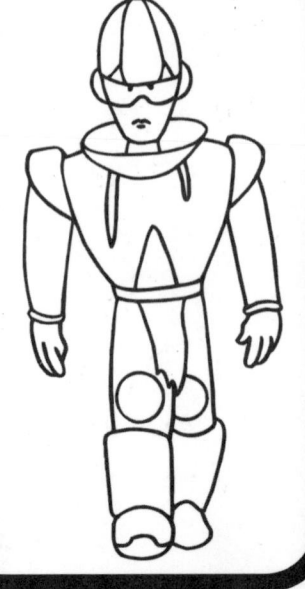  

Super Lady · Jaws

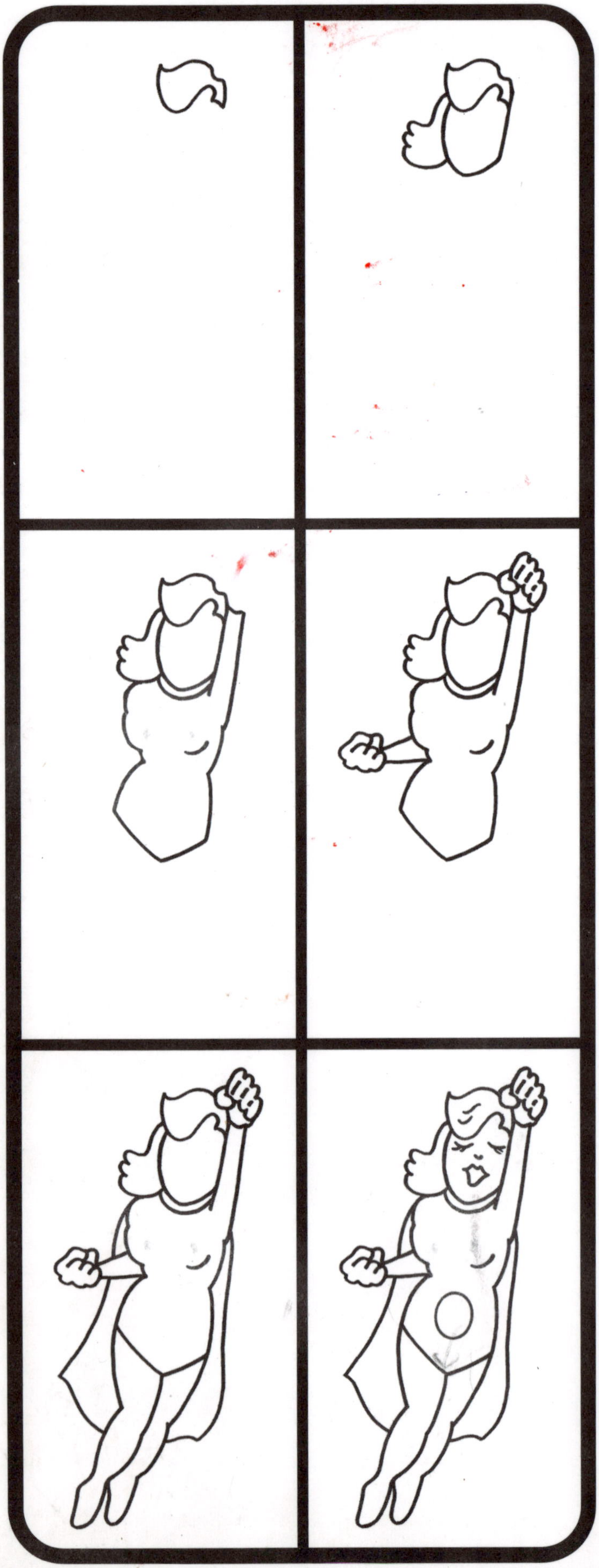

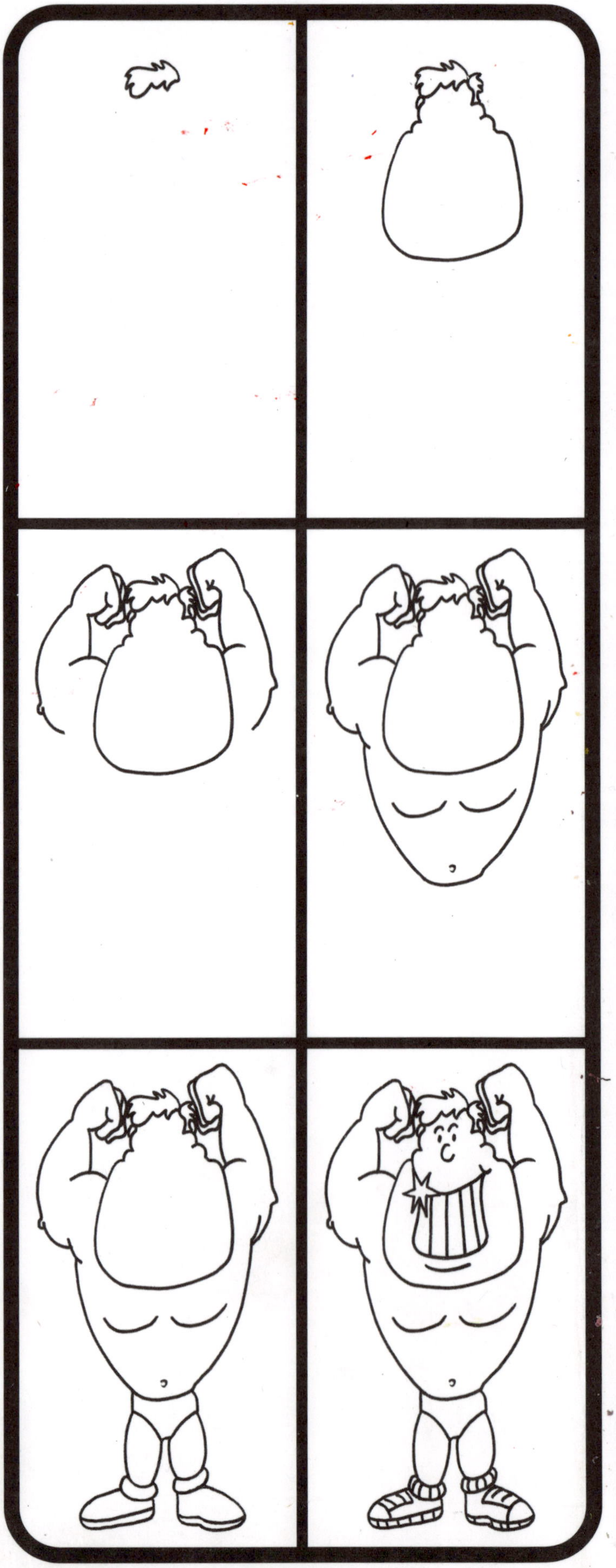

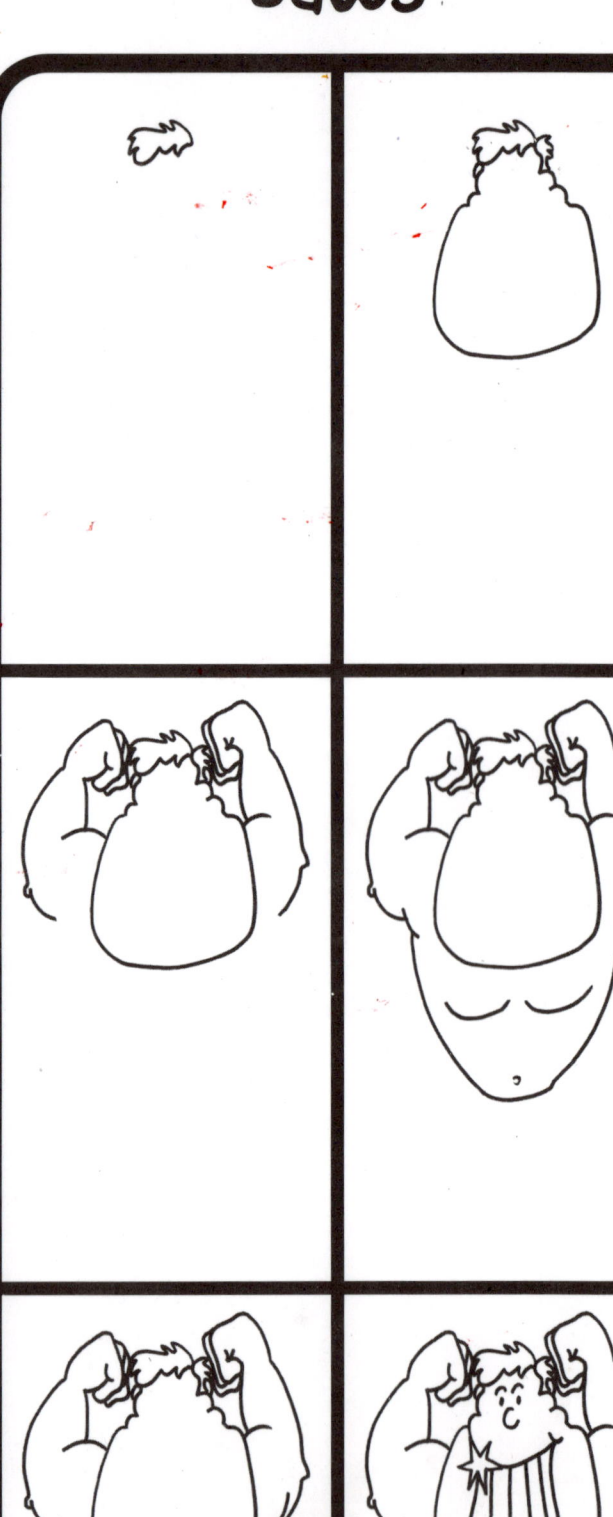

Super Thor   Super caveman

Blade Warrior   Celtic Warrior

Sir-Lance-A-Lot

Hannibal

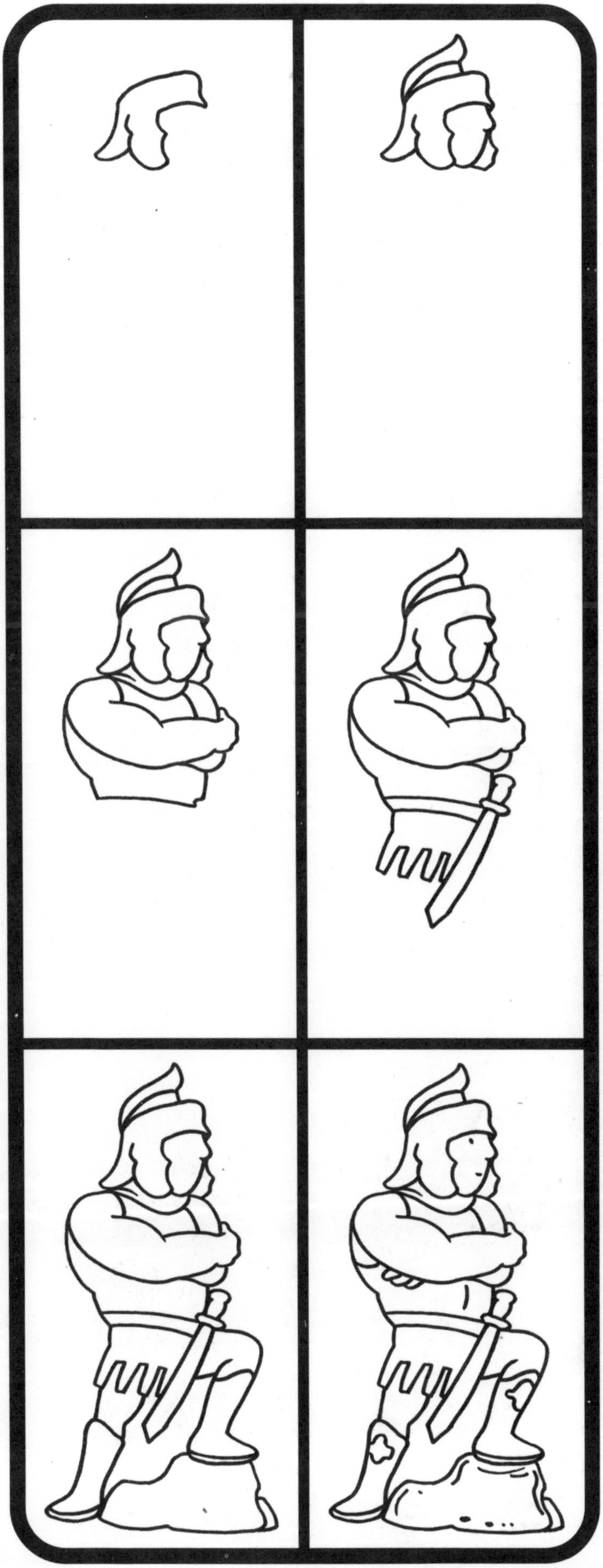

Super Moose

Volgan

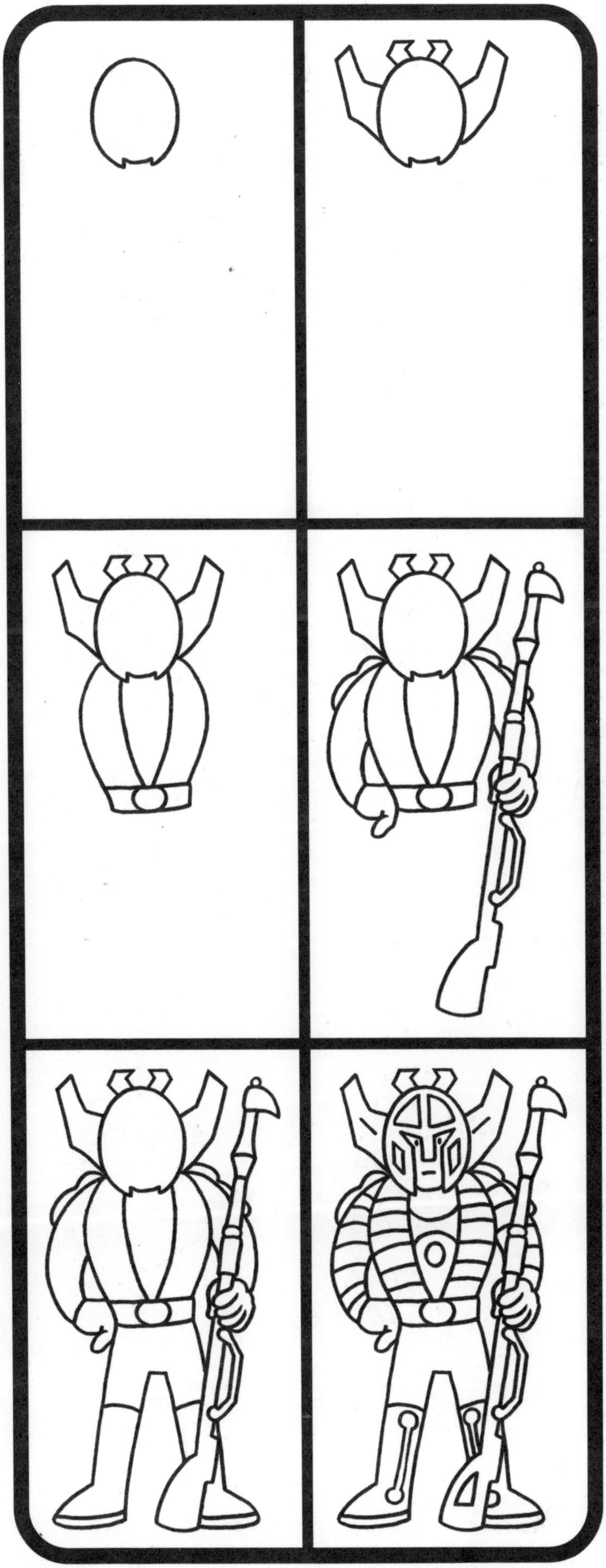

Buffalo Bill

Galactica

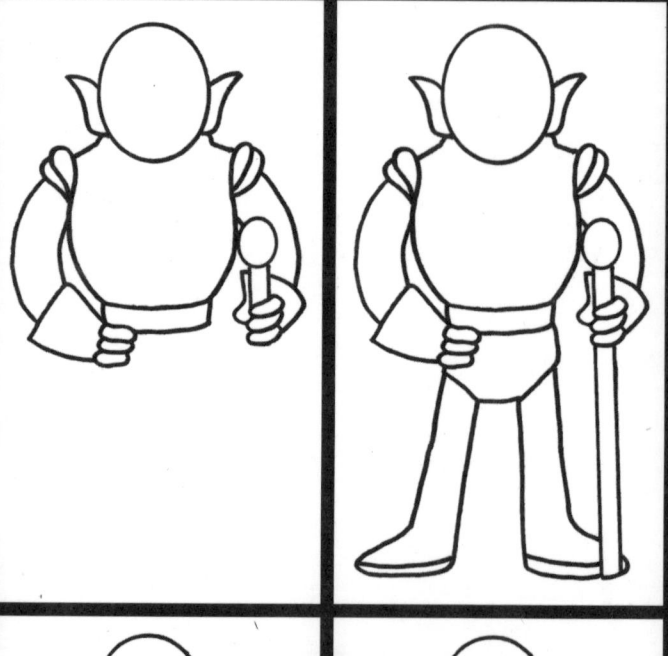
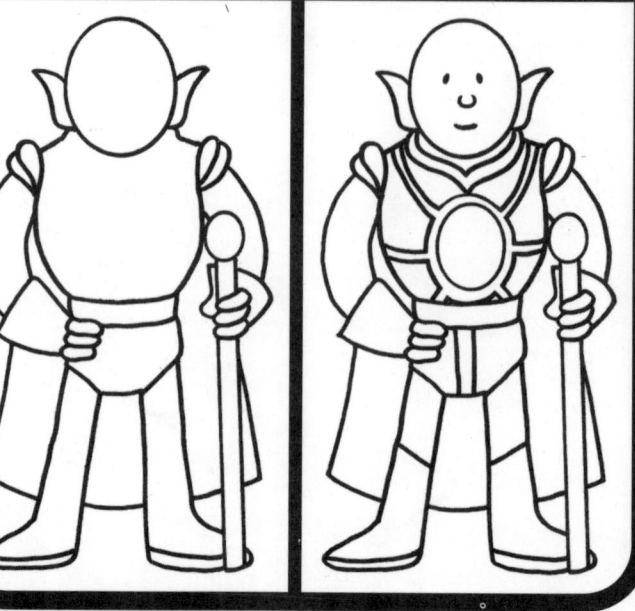

Super oil

Rope Breaker

The Bat # Globe Man

Space Robot

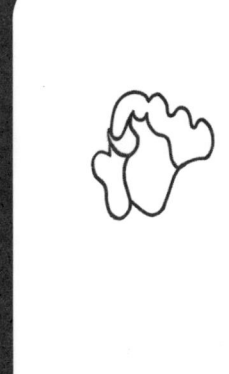

Space Baroness

Space Warrior   Sonic Hero

Mechanic Man

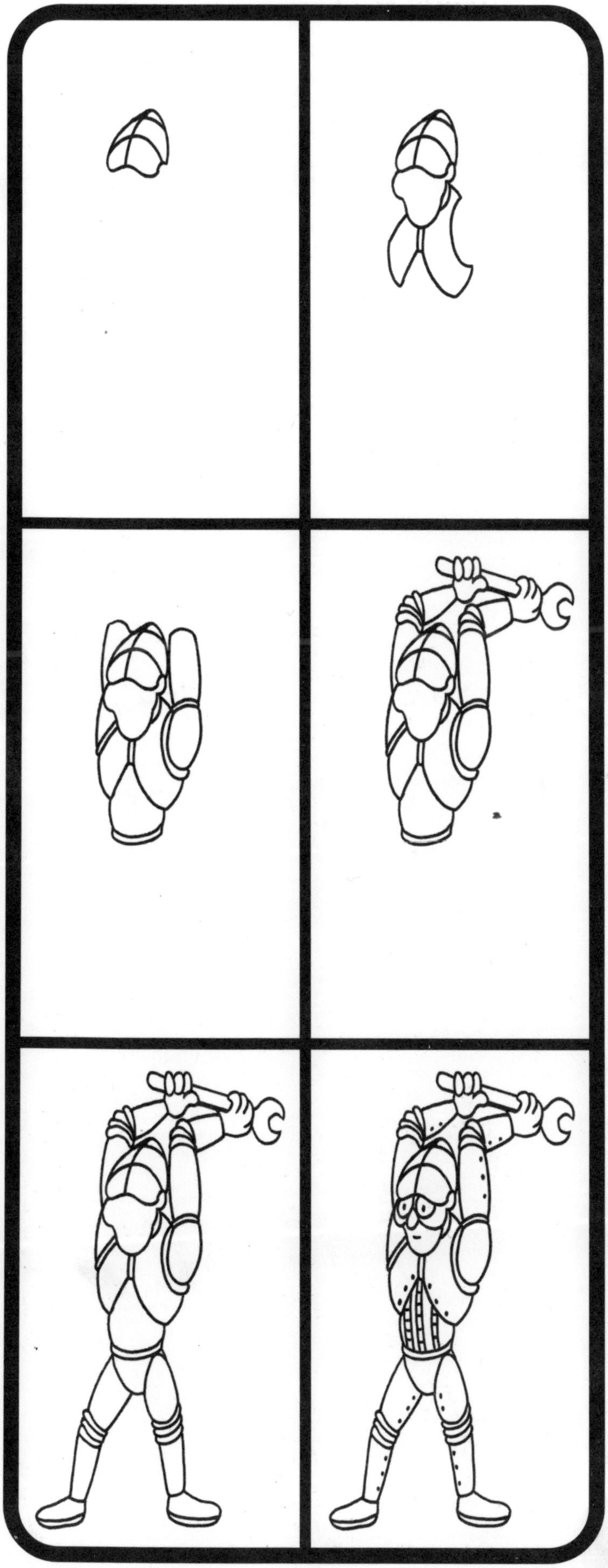

Demon Fighter

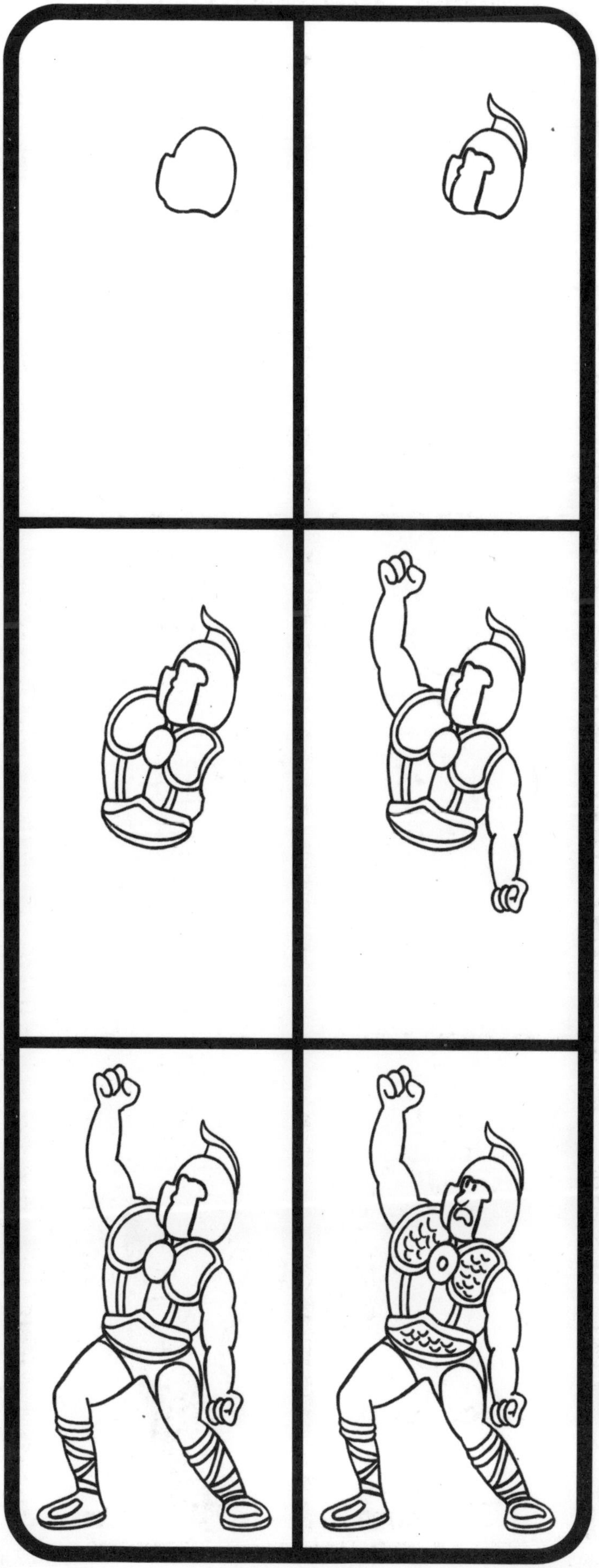

Demon Slayer

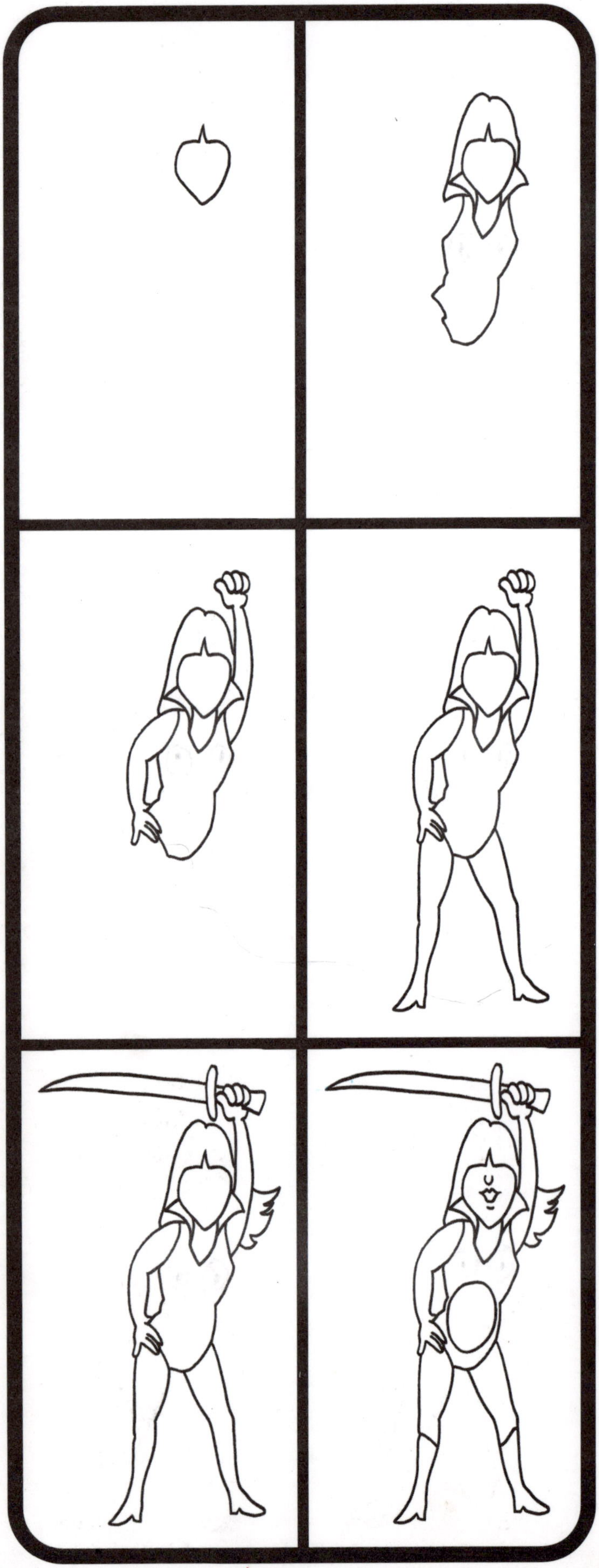

Lightning Diver

UDDz   captain Galactic

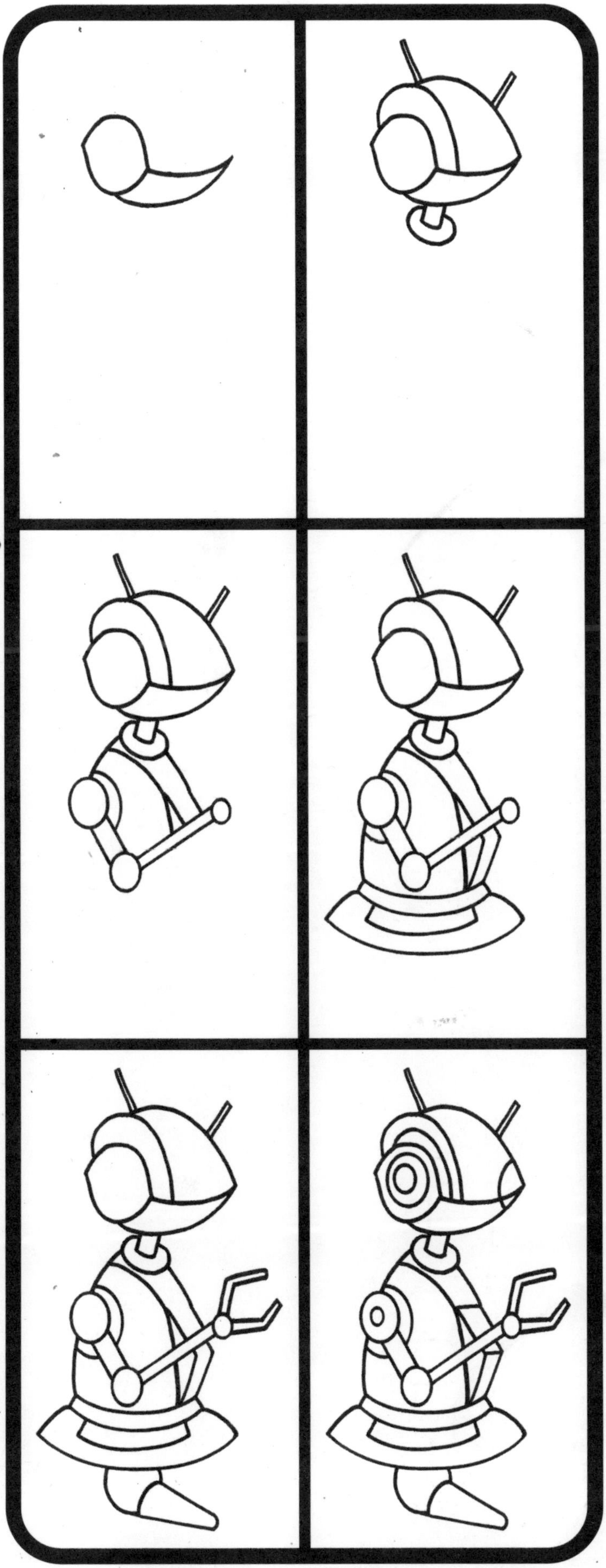

Ninja   Axeman

The Archer   Lightning

Sky Boxer

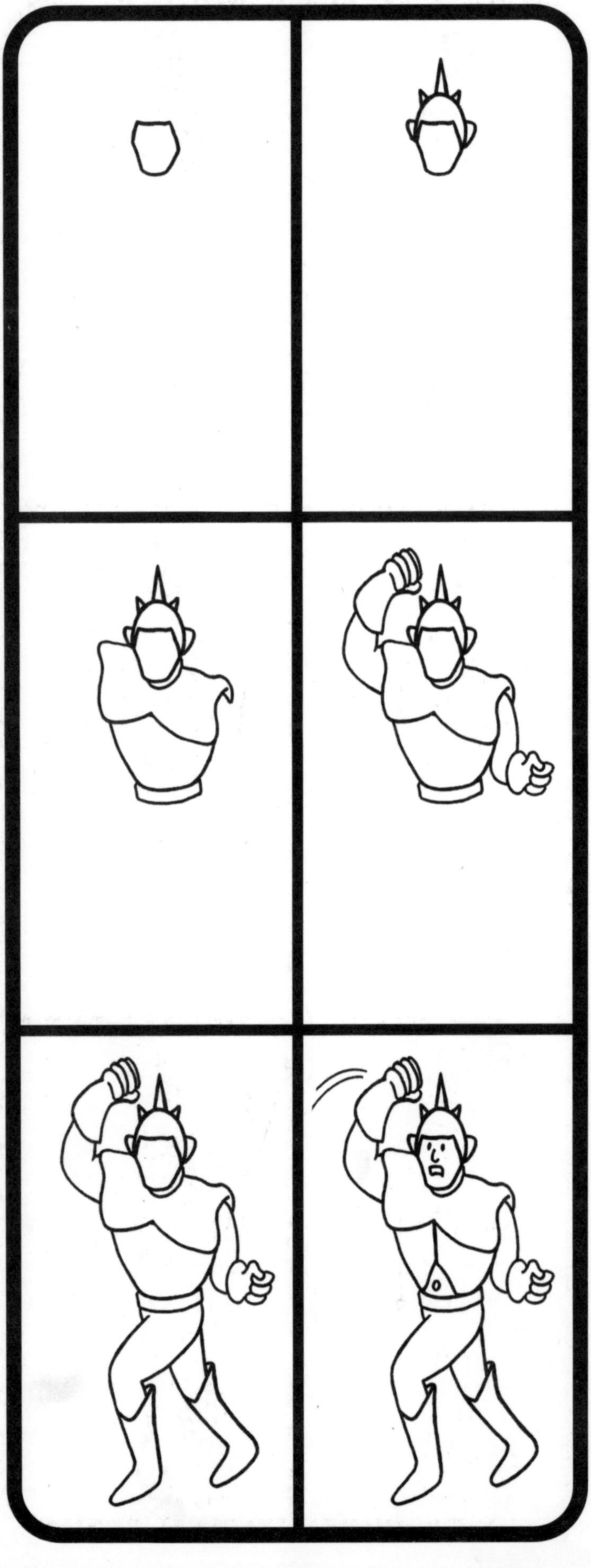

Venus Amazon

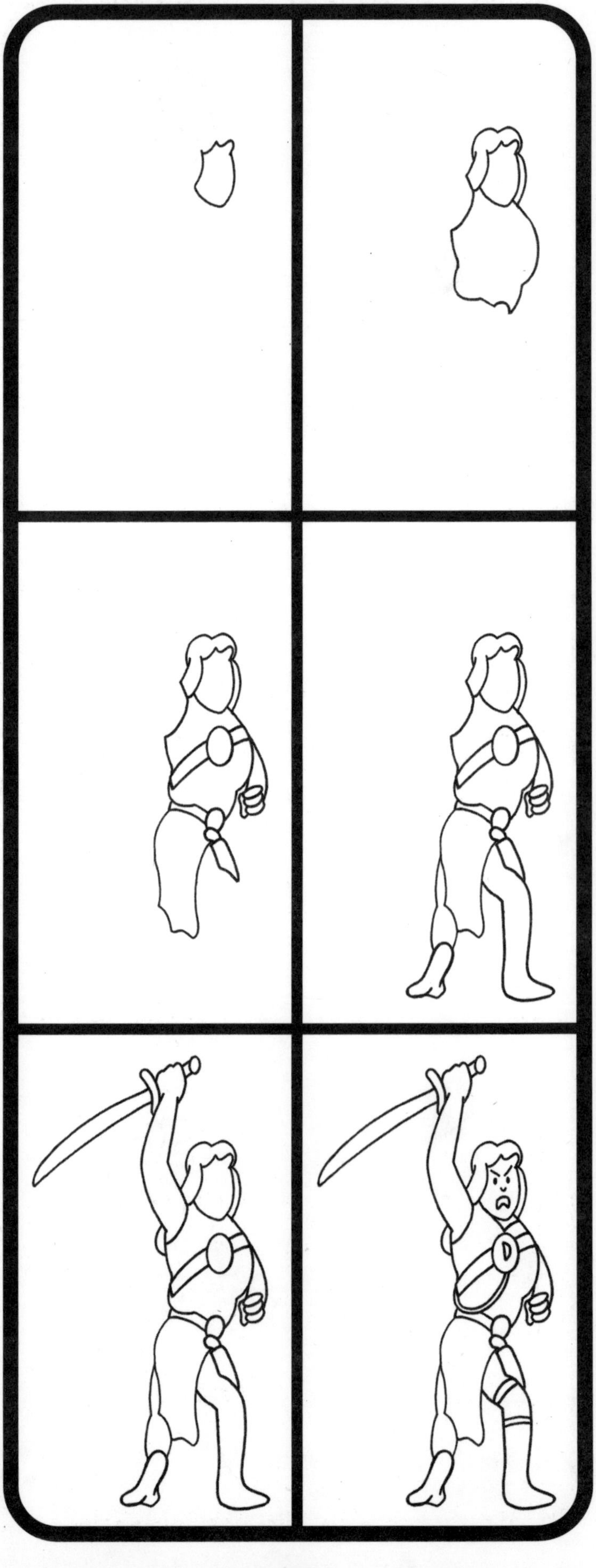

Star Warden   Spartacus

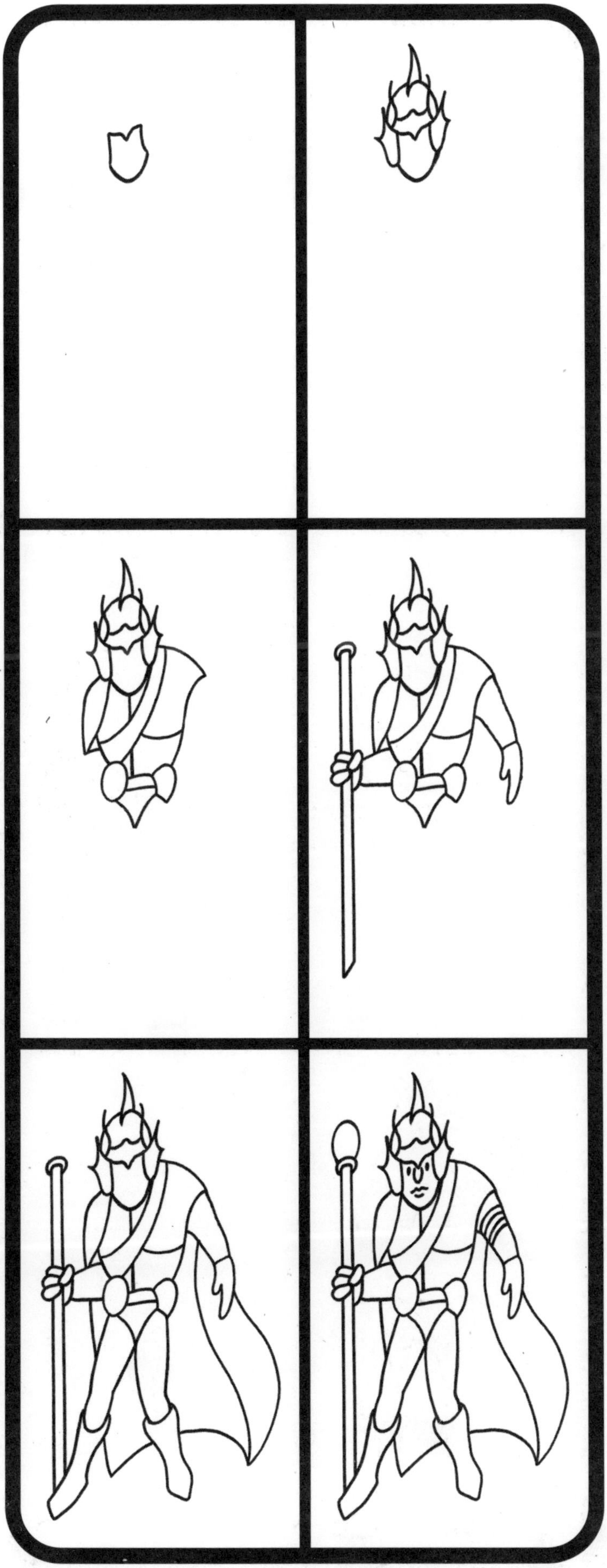

Star Hunter Space Shield

Kajo　　Zulu

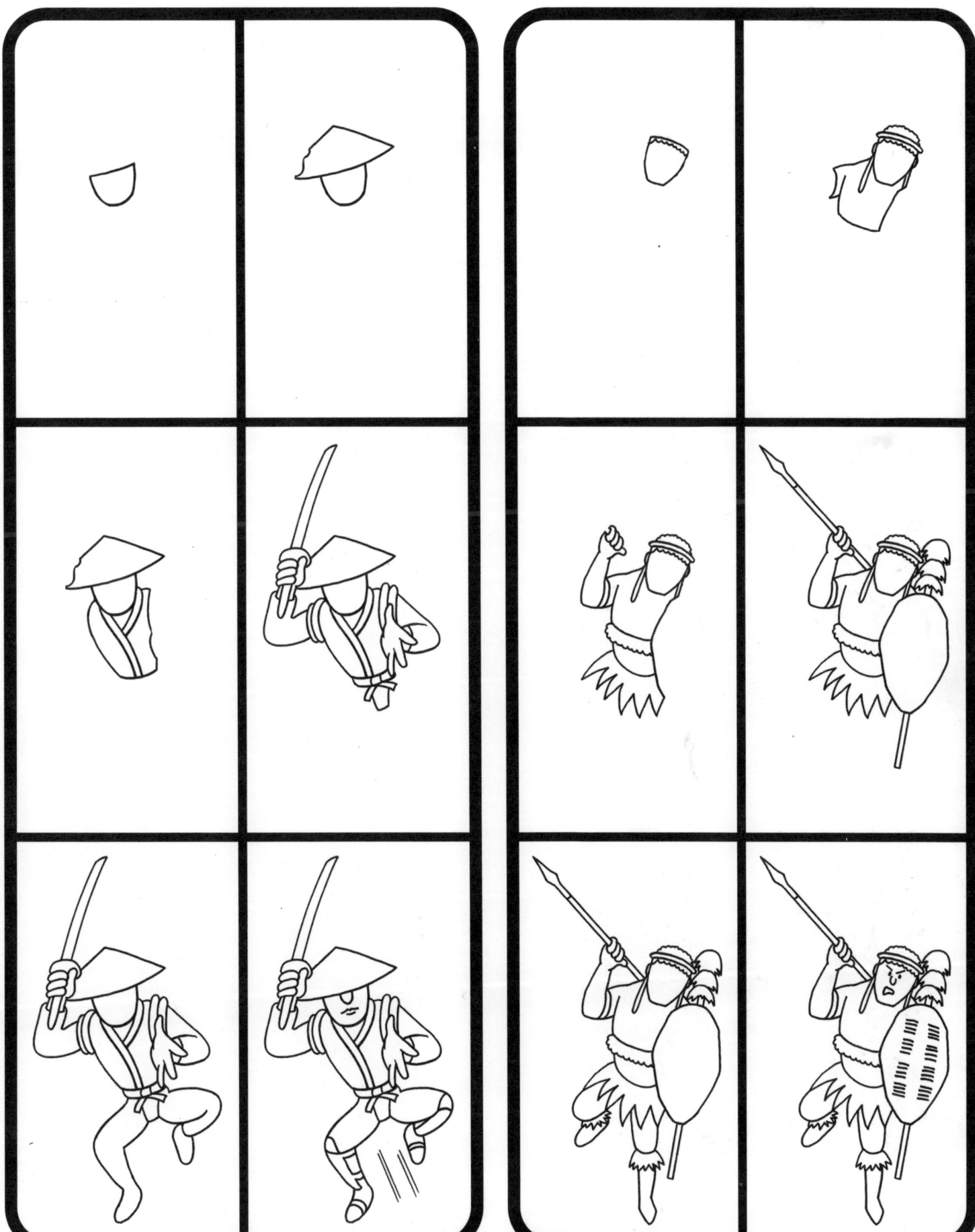

Robot Warrior   Frogman

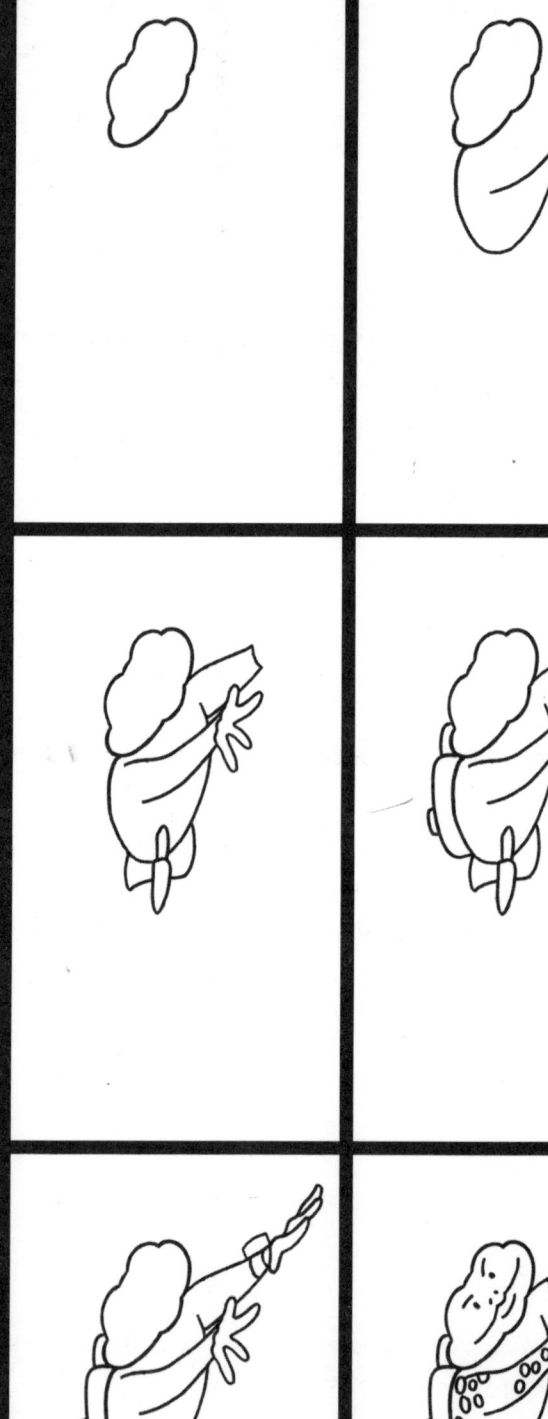

Space Sniper

Prince Sword

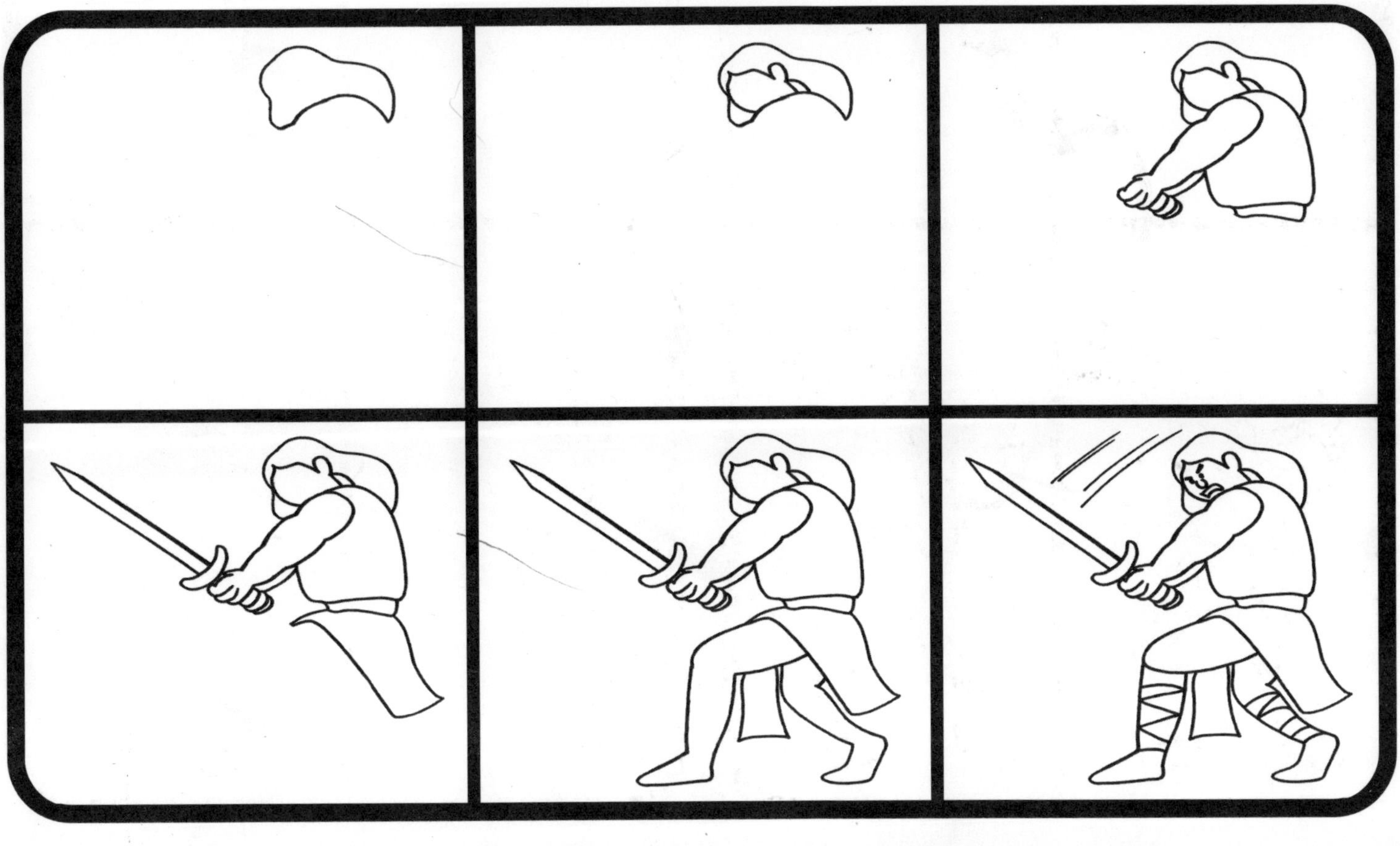

Karate King

Sky Diver

Super Saver

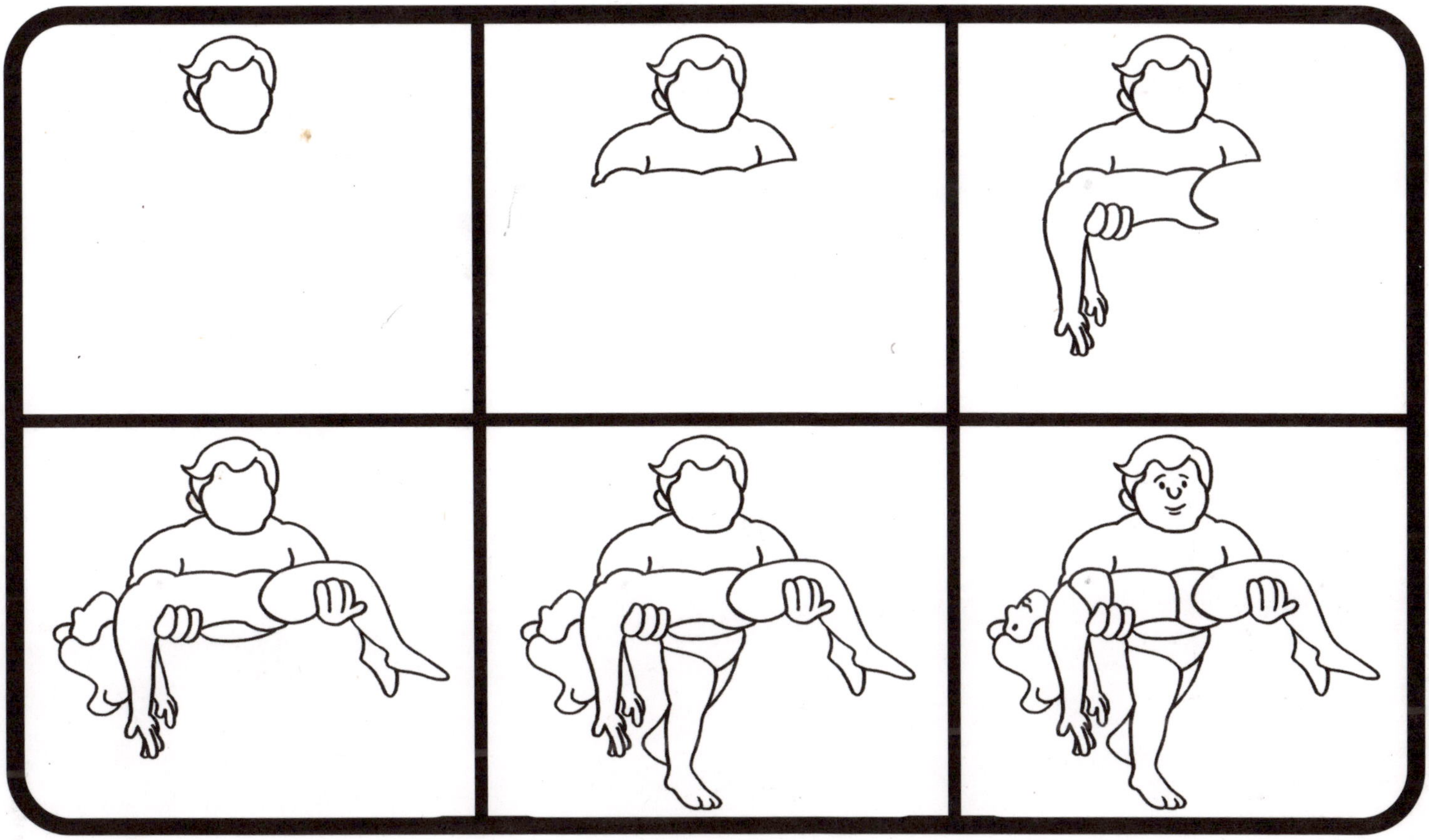

Samurai

Queen Boudicca

Aztec

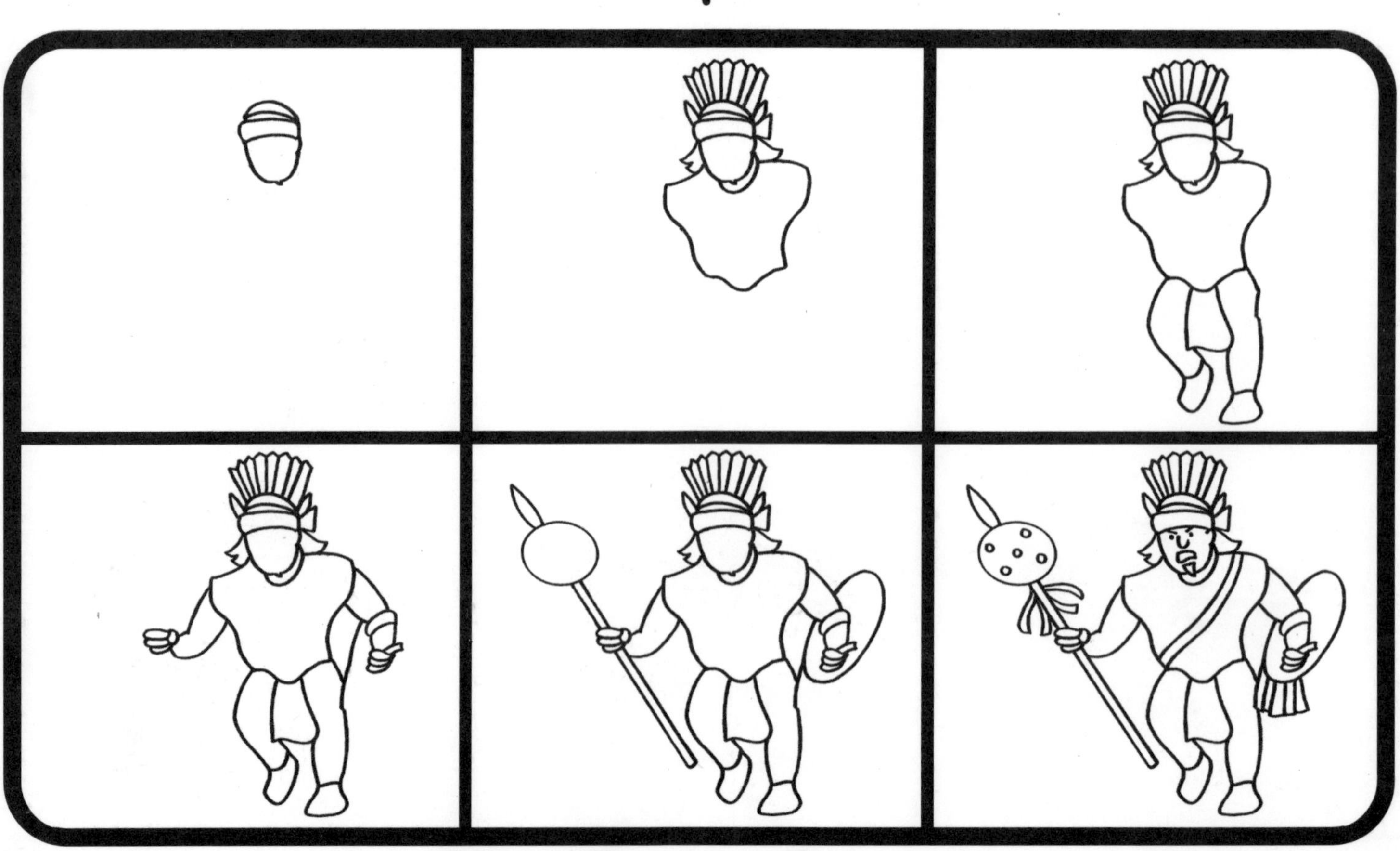

Super Star

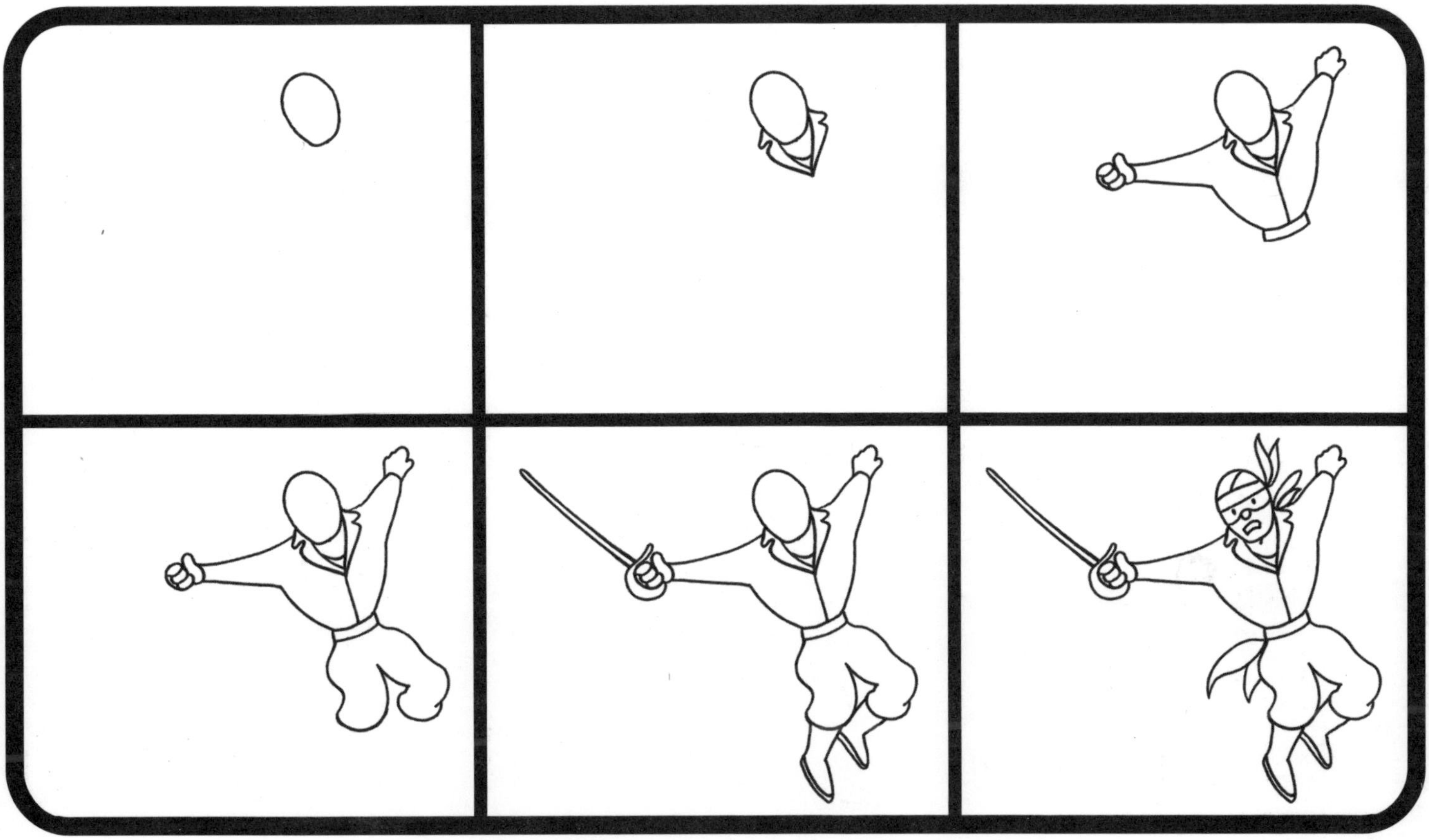

Sky Leaper

Swash Buccaneer

Space Skater

Lizardus

Surf Boarder

Super Egor

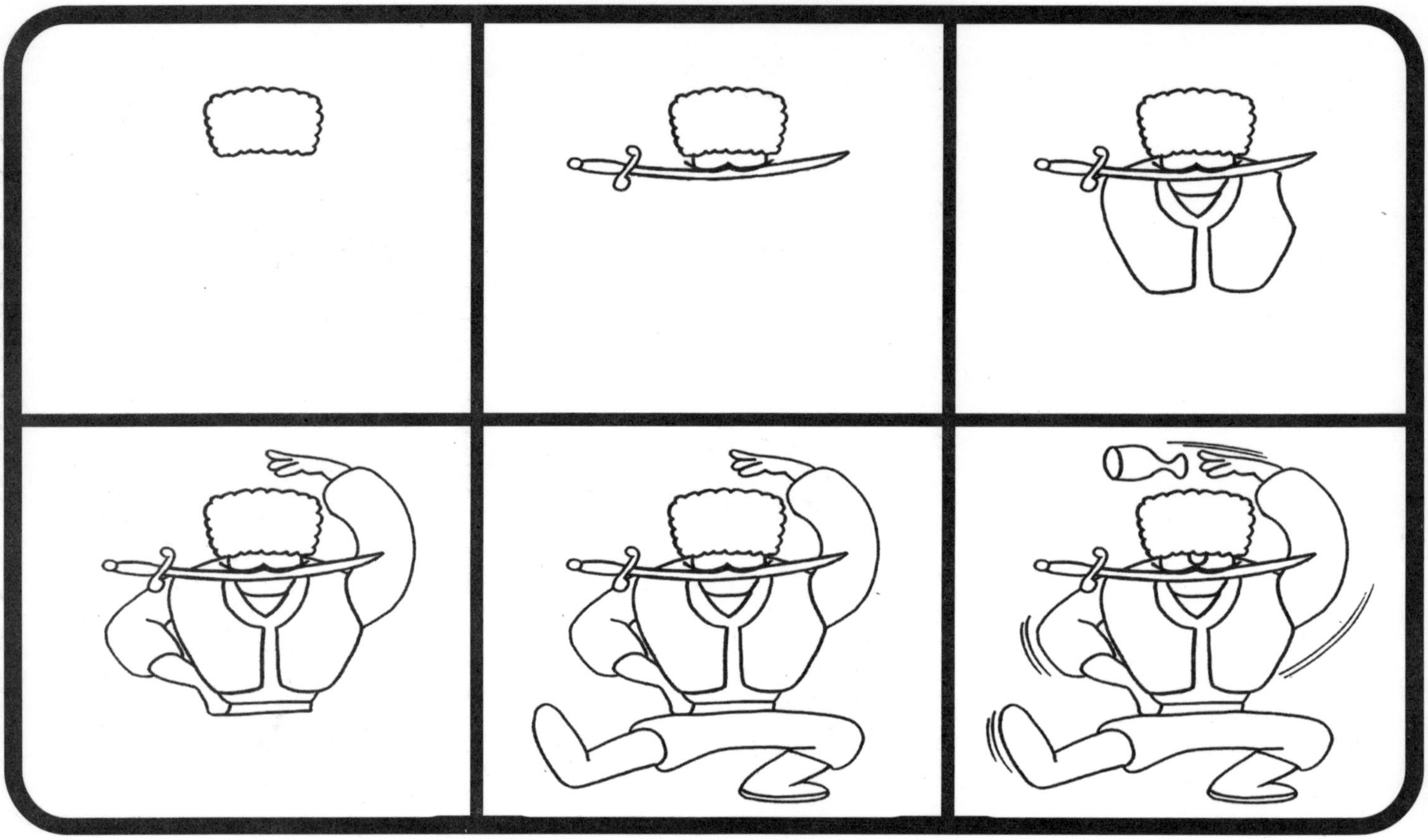

Skater

Space Queen

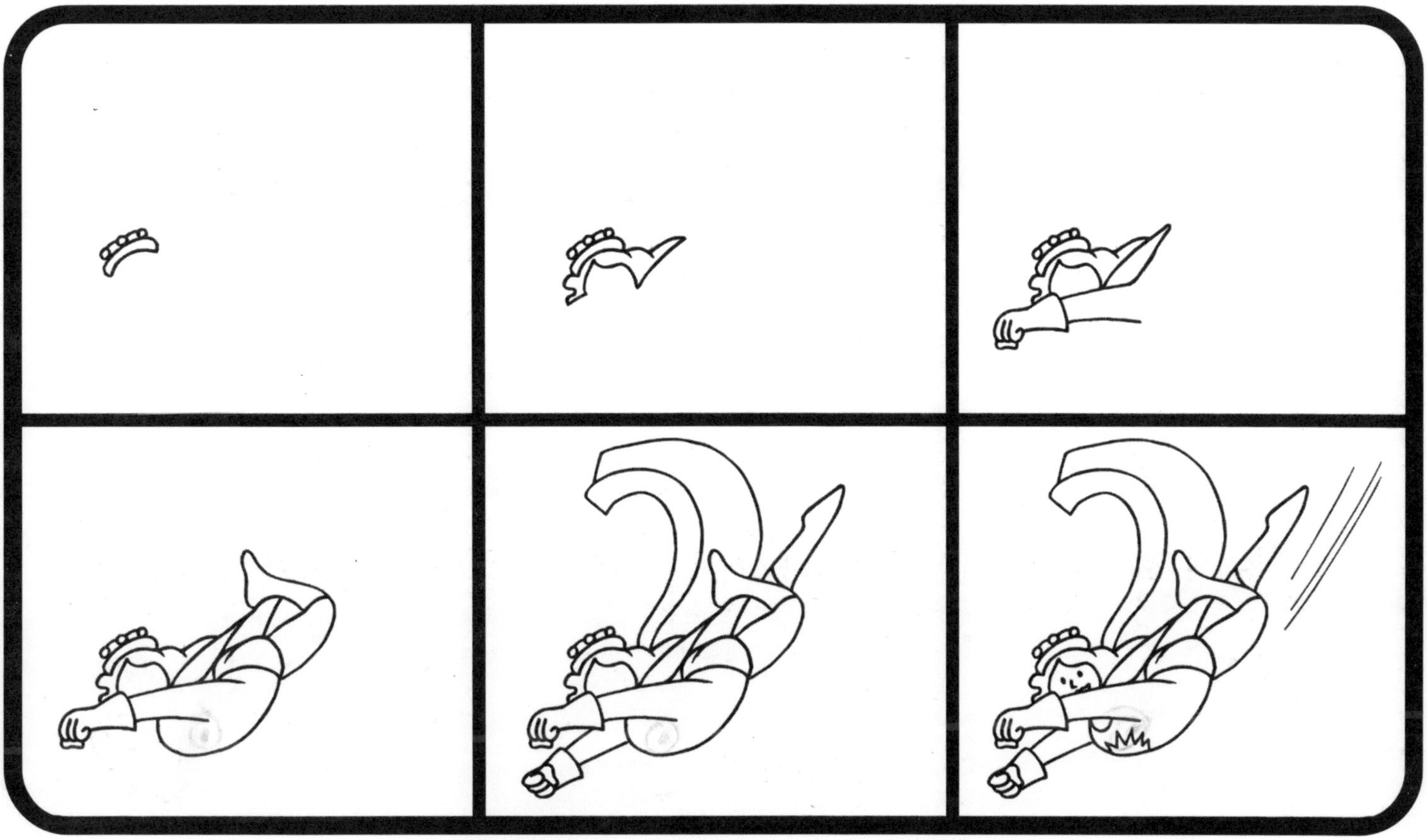

Super Charger

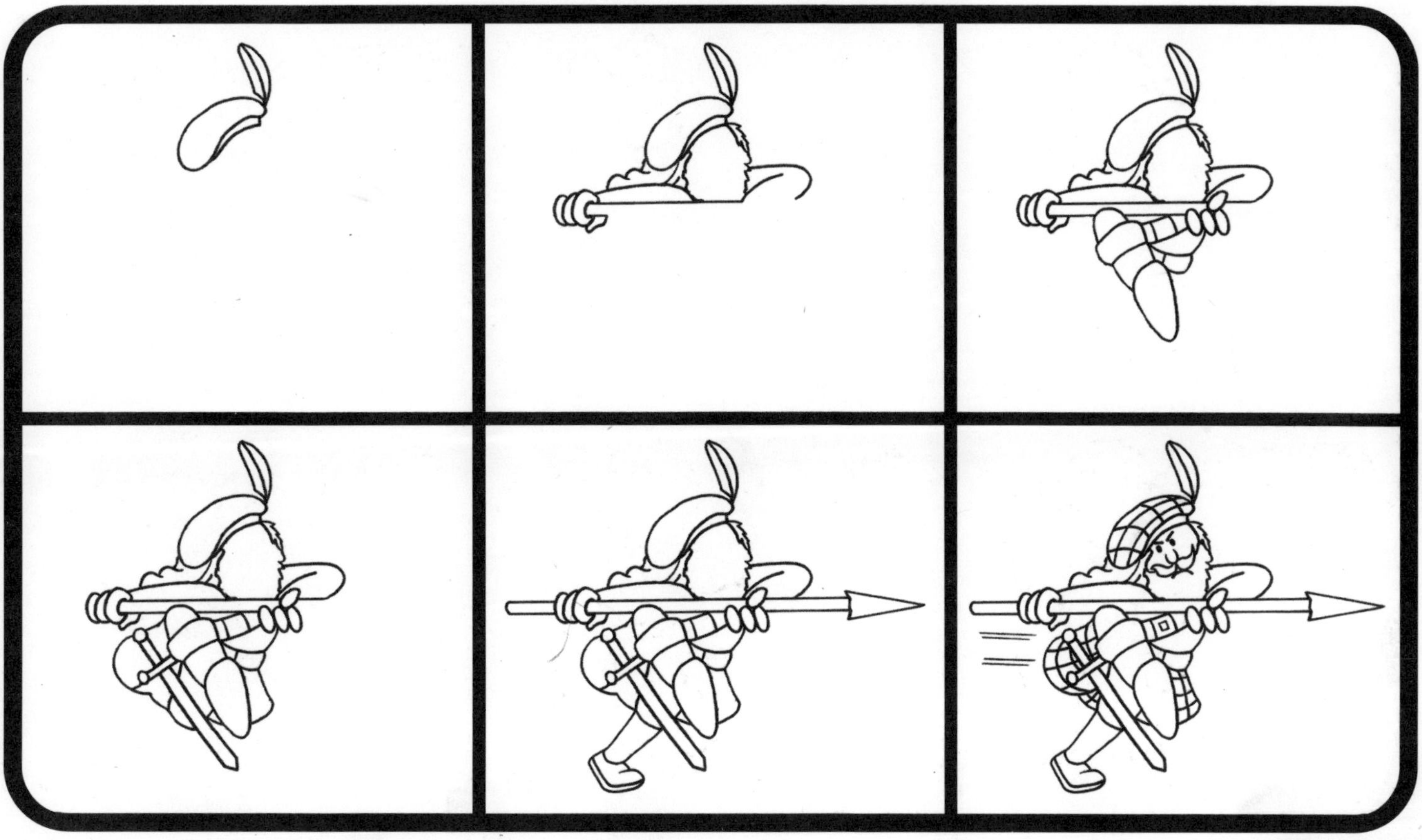

G.I.

Markovian Lancer

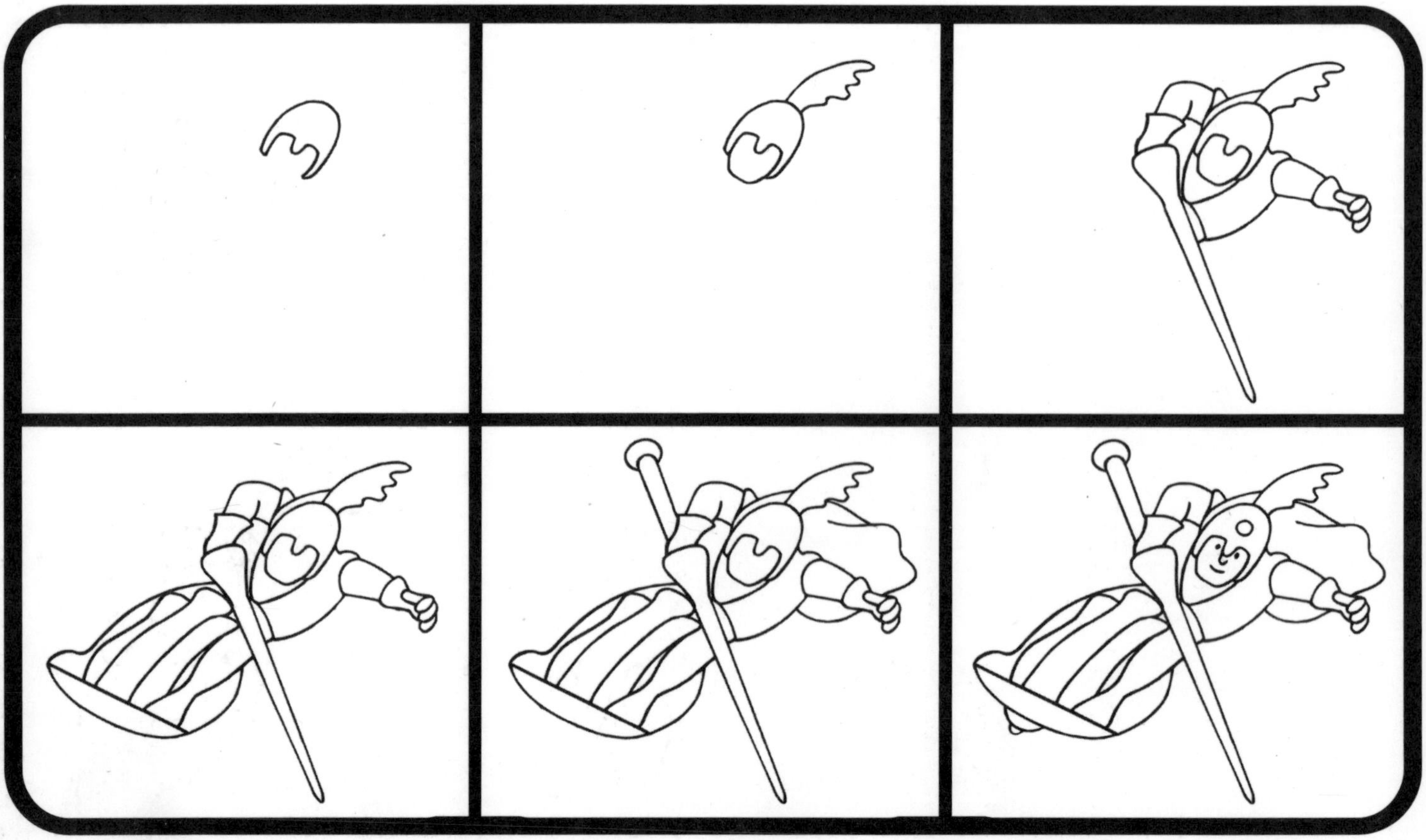

Greek Hero

Sky Scraper

Robo

Kango Kicker

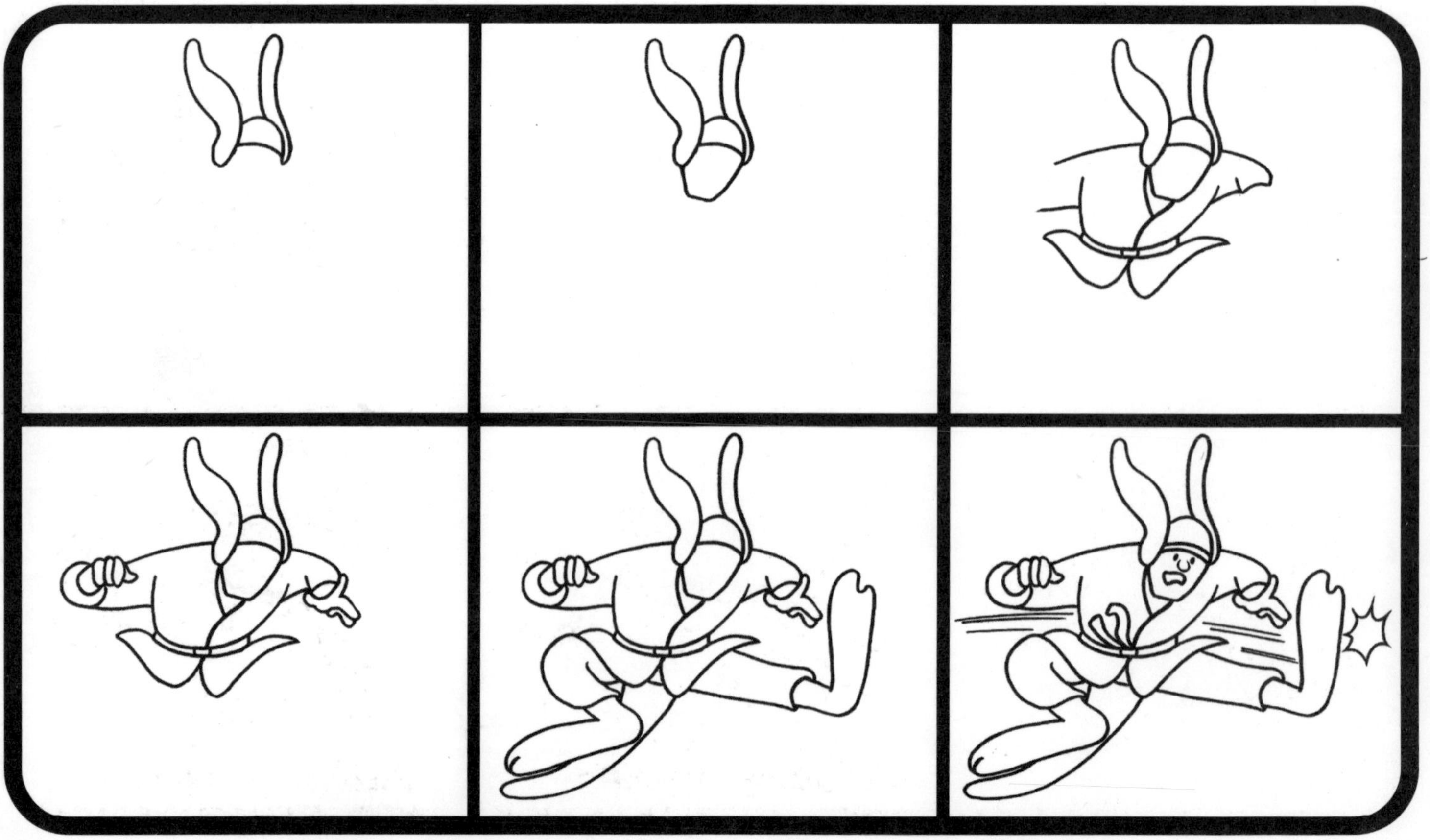

Star Chaser

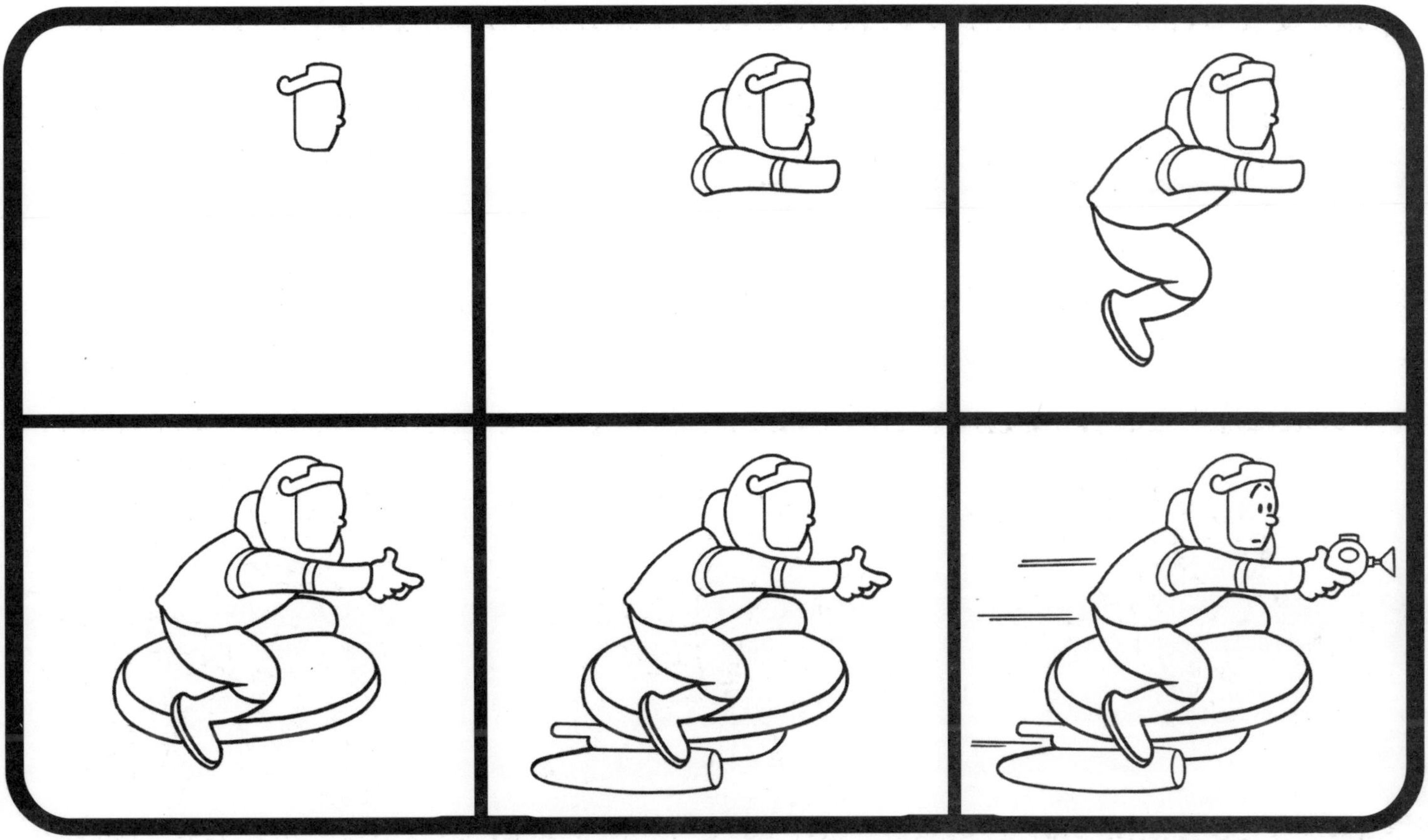

Rocky Hunter

Super Power

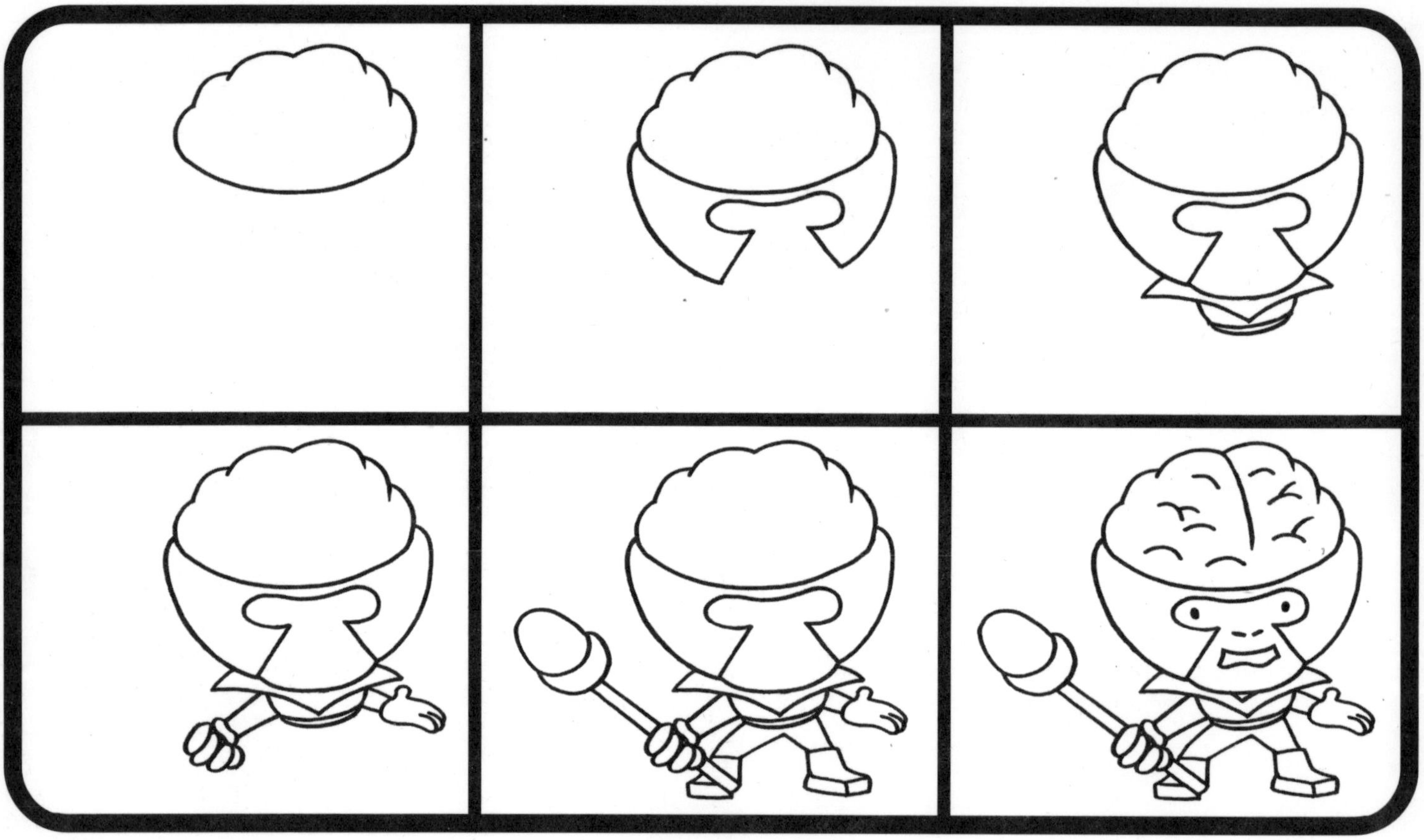

Android

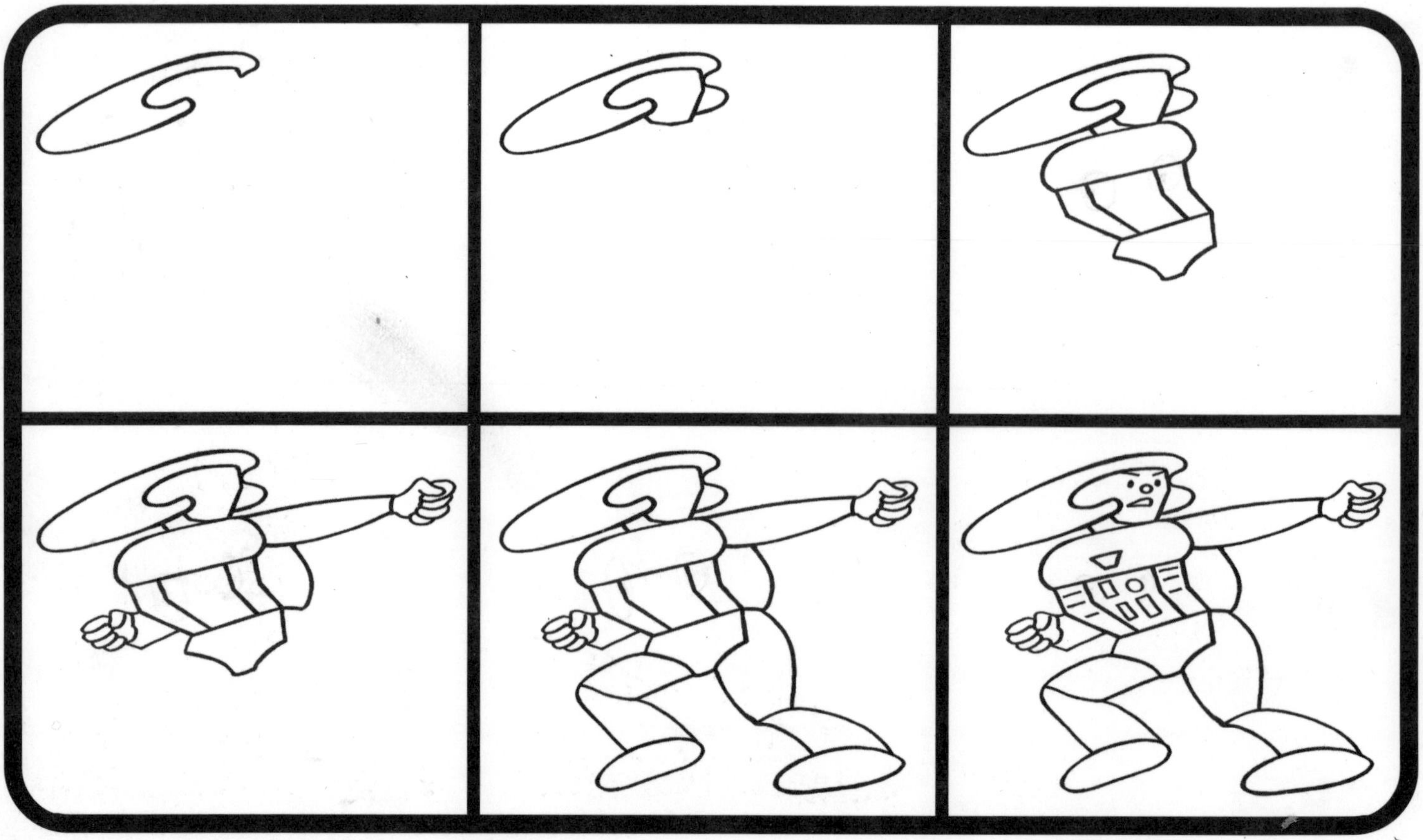

Super Silly-us

Kongo

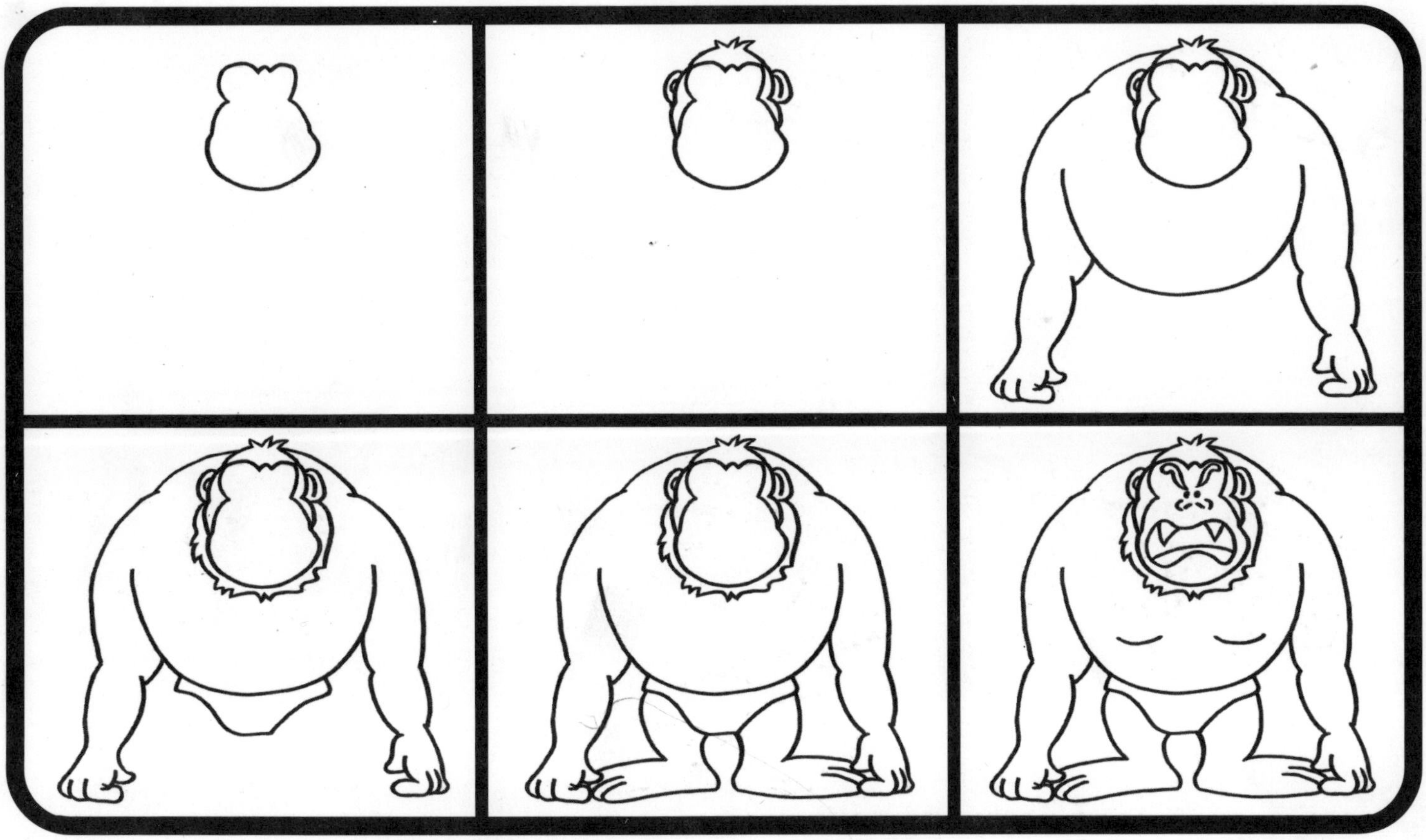

Star Skater

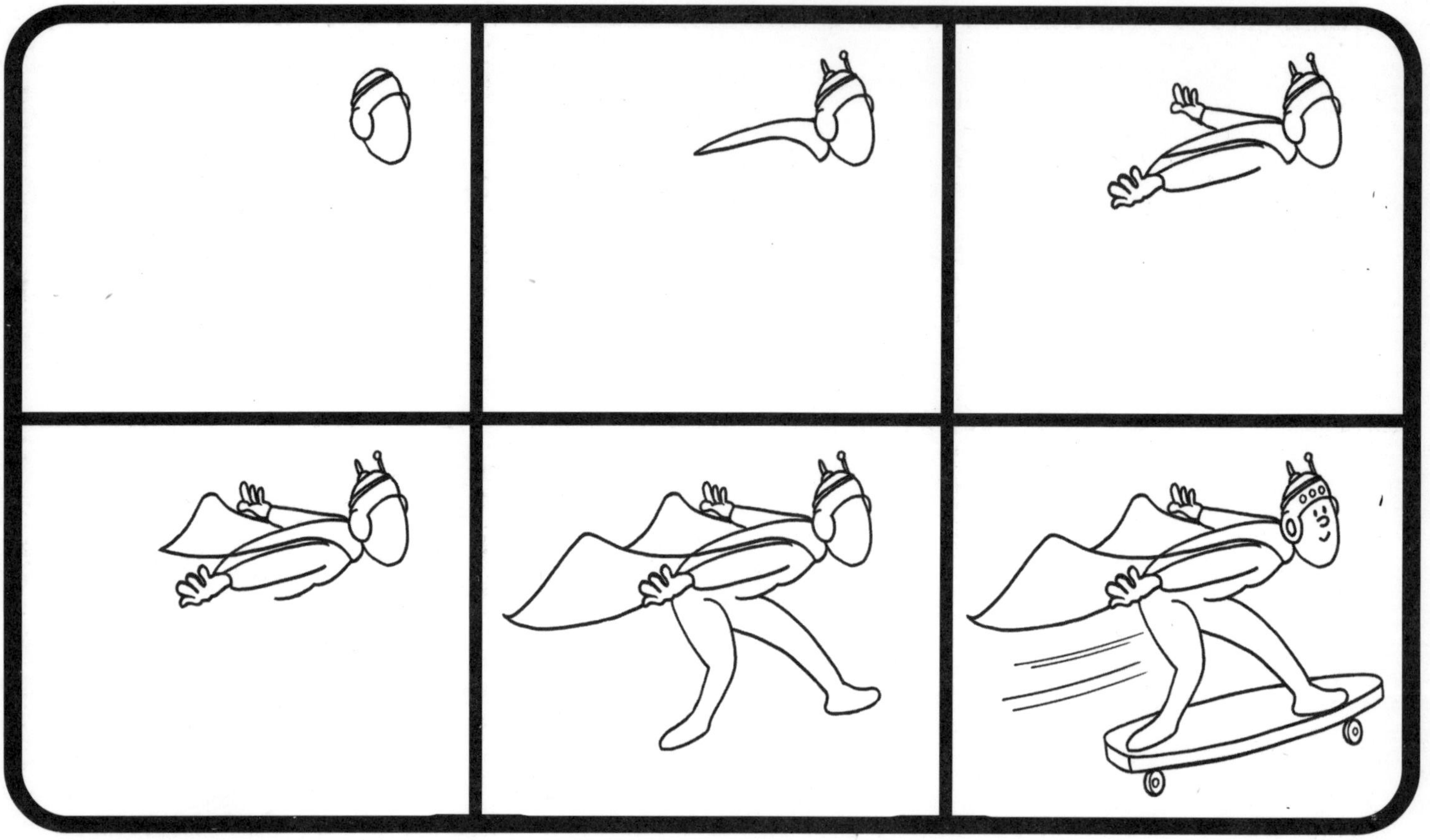

Arachnia

Layzar

Super Swooper

Super Nan

Barbarus

Super Flyer

Space Lancer

Super Spy

Goliath

Sitting Bull

Super Strongman

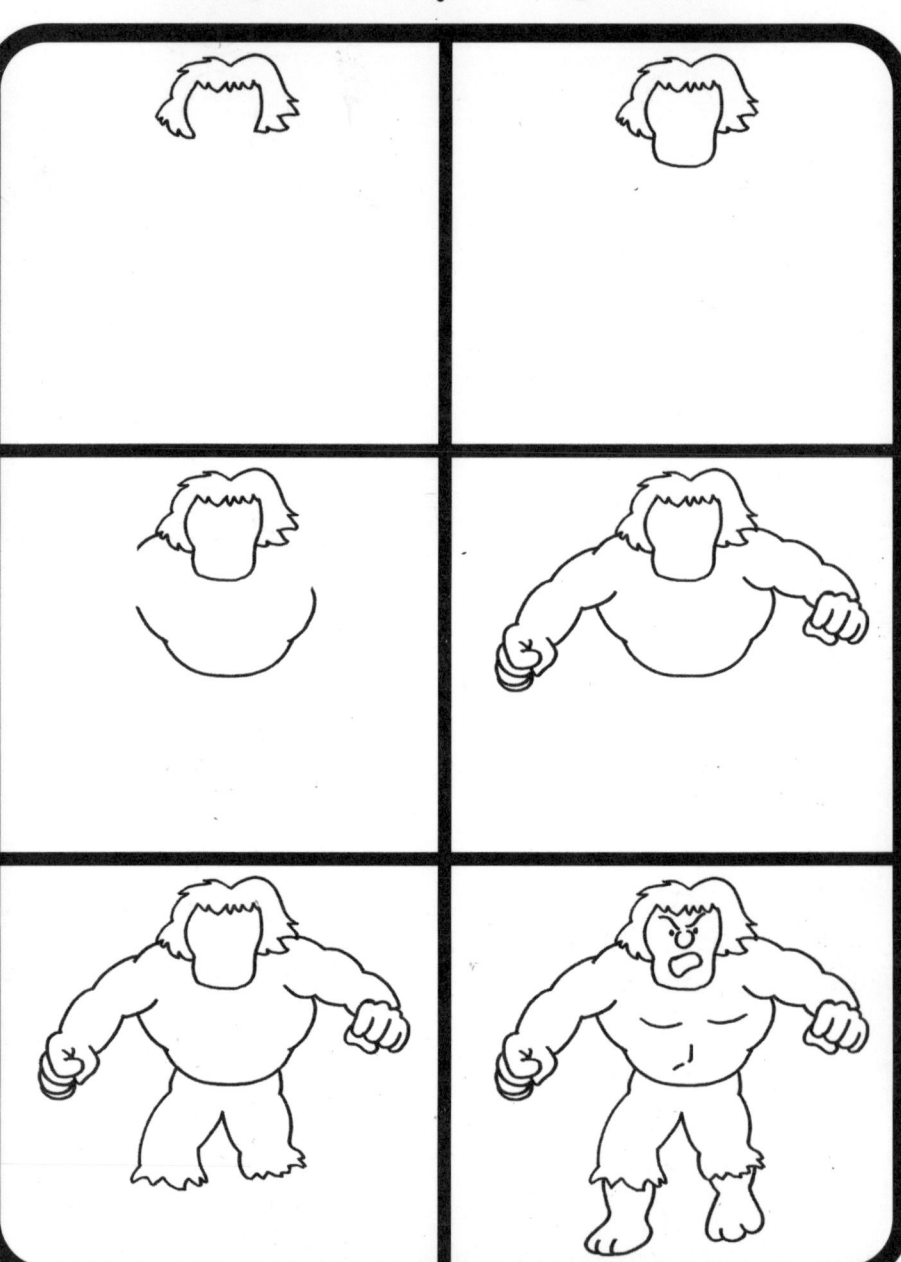

Space Saver

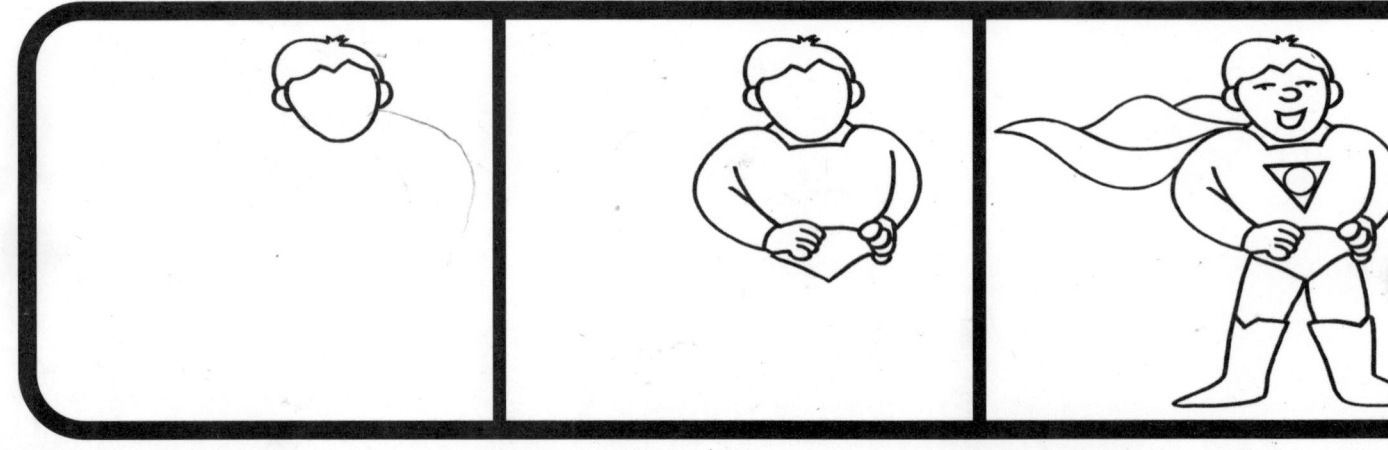

Iron Man

Super Boy

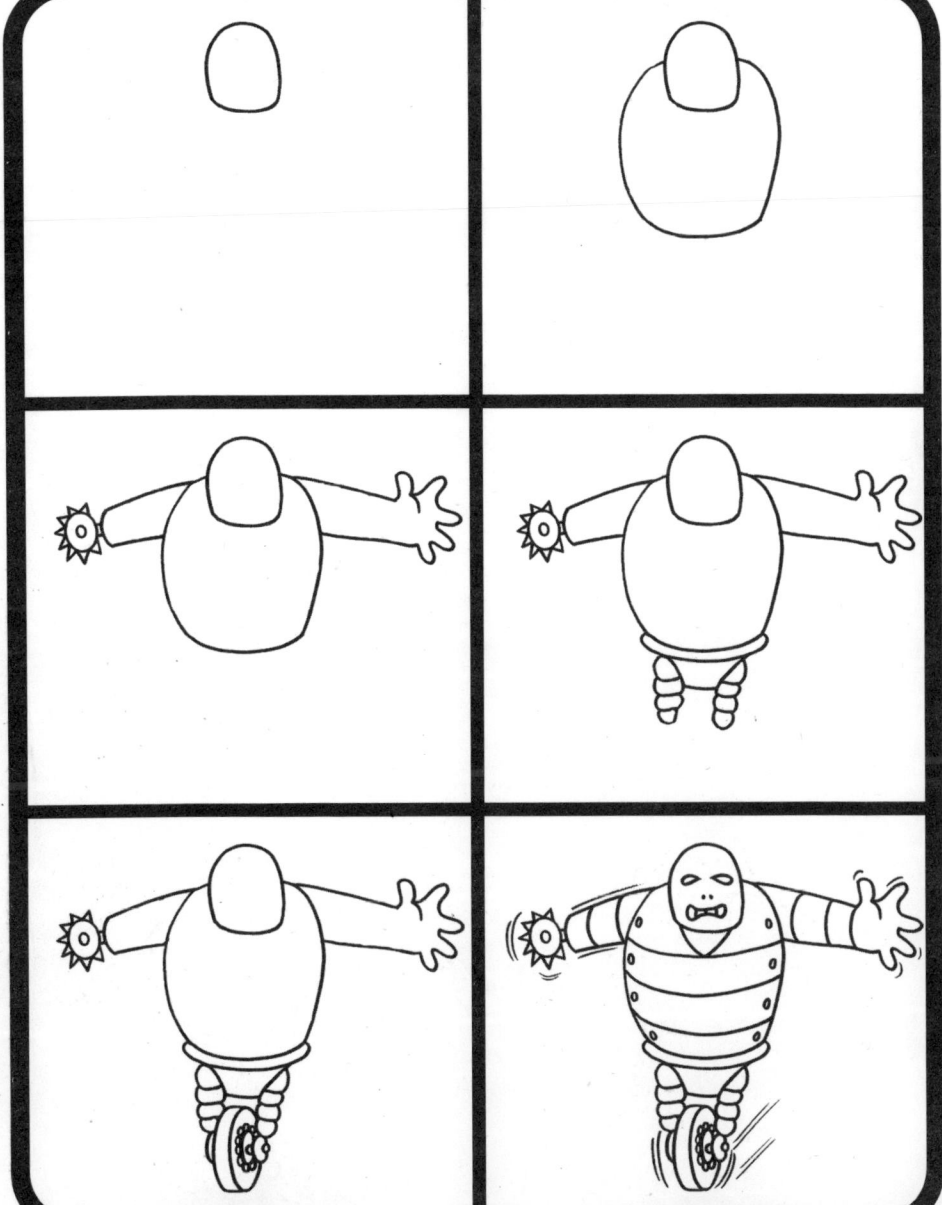
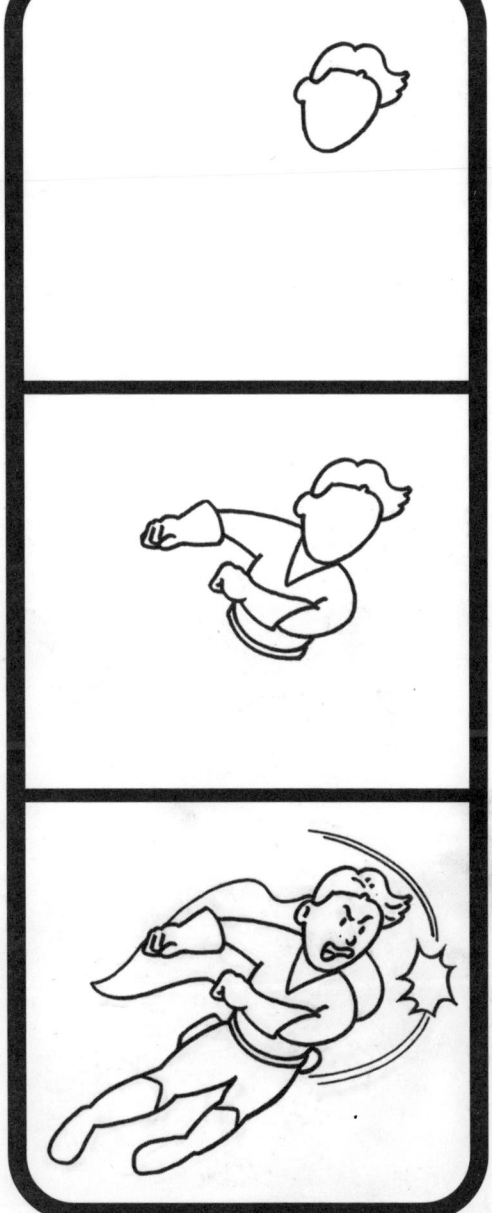

Super Woof

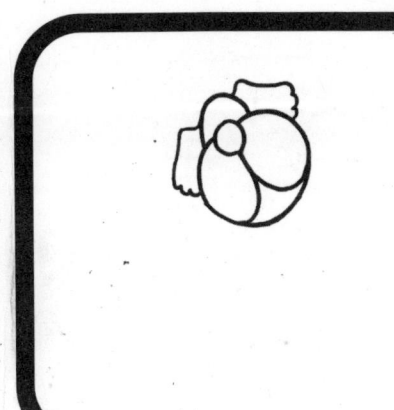

Super Bunny

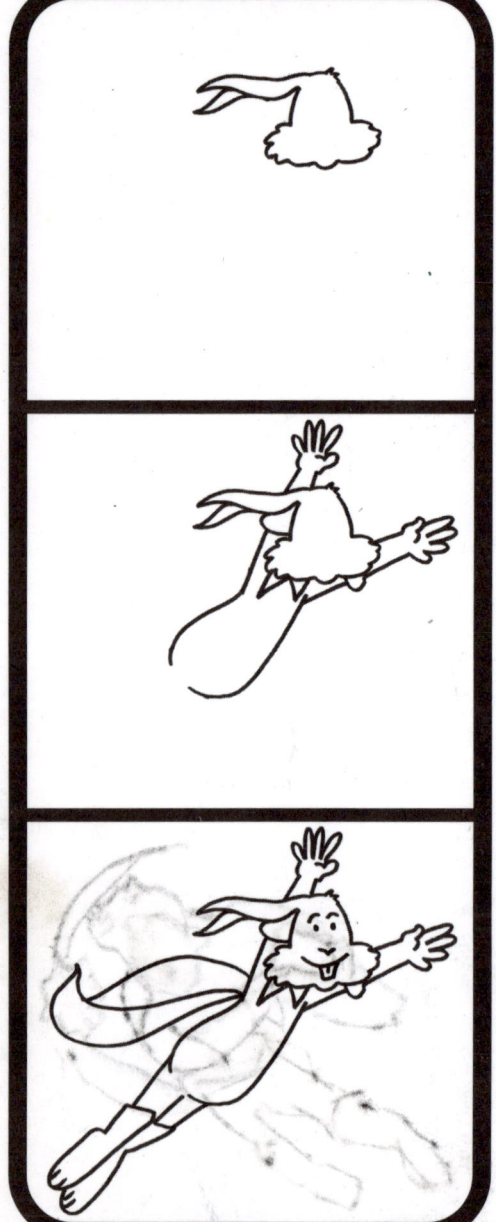

Big Beard

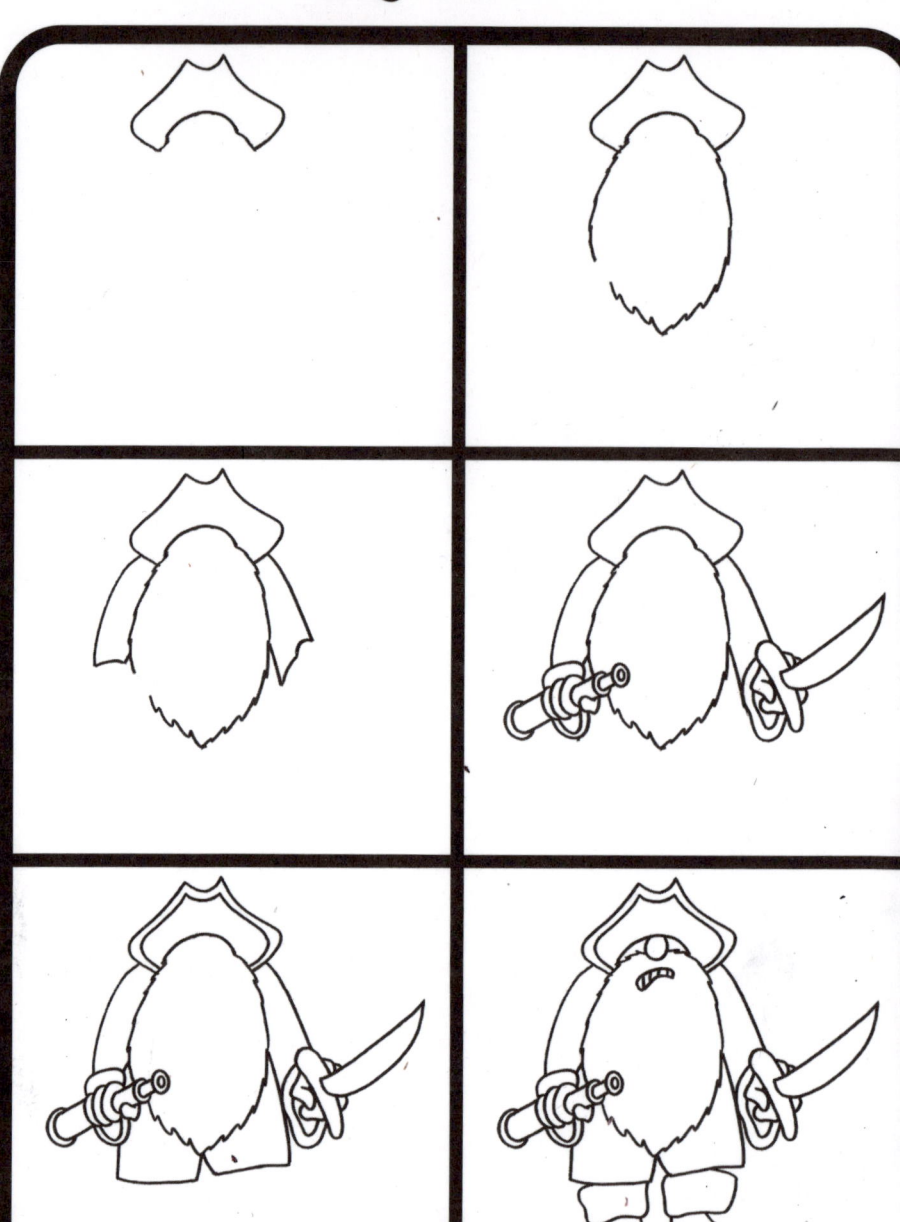

Mighty Mog